PHANTOM WRITER 6

TYNDALE HOUSE PUBLISHERS, INC., CAROL STREAM, ILLINOIS

JERRY B. JENKINS · CHRIS FABRY

Visit Tyndale's exciting Web site for kids at www.tyndale.com/kids.

TYNDALE is a registered trademark of Tyndale House Publishers, Inc.

The Tyndale Kids logo is a trademark of Tyndale House Publishers, Inc.

Phantom Writer

Designed by Jacqueline L. Nuñez

Edited by Lorie Popp

Published in association with the literary agency of Alive Communications, Inc., 7680 Goddard Street, Suite 200, Colorado Springs, CO 80920.

For manufacturing information regarding this product, please call 1-800-323-9400.

Library of Congress Cataloging-in-Publication Data

Jenkins, Jerry B.
    Phantom writer / Jerry B. Jenkins, Chris Fabry.
       p. cm. — (Red Rock mysteries ; 6)
       ISBN 978-1-4143-0145-7 (sc)
    [1. Authorship—Fiction.   2. Missing persons—Fiction.   3. Christian life—Fiction.   4. Twins—Fiction.   5. Family life—Colorado—Fiction.   6. Colorado—Fiction.   7. Mystery and detective stories.]   I. Fabry, Chris, date.   II. Title.   III. Series: Jenkins, Jerry B. Red Rock mysteries ; 6

    PZ7.J4138Ph 2005
    [Fic]—dc22   2005008025

Printed in the United States of America

17   16   15   14
 9   8   7   6   5   4

"People say I'm **STRANGE,**
that I have a **WEIRD BRAIN.** It's not true.
I have a **PERFECTLY FINE**-looking brain
that I keep in a bottle of formaldehyde
on my bookshelf."

Jake Konig

"**WRITING** is **HARD WORK**
and **BAD** for your **HEALTH.**"
E. B. White

CHAPTER 1

☻ *Bryce* ☻

Everybody has a secret. Mine is Jake Konig.

Jake makes money from nightmares and screams. Lots of money. For the past few years he's kept millions of kids and adults up all hours of the night with his creepy books. I'm one of them, but only my family knows.

I know what Jake looks like from the pictures on his books. Leather jacket pulled up around his neck. Tight jeans that make his lanky legs look like pythons. Little kids get out of the way when they see him coming, and those who don't, he pushes out of the way.

My twin sister, Ashley, doesn't read the books. She says they're too scary. She won't even look at the covers, with their 3-D faces and spooky houses. At Halloween, kids dress up as characters from the books. Ashley thinks it's disgusting, but I think it's cool.

My favorite is the one about the kid who gets trapped in a dungeon and has to figure his way out. There are several tunnels, and if he chooses the wrong one, a gigantic spider will chase him or a boulder the size of our house will crush him. Only one path leads outside. That's like what the Bible says about finding God, that there's only one path, but Ashley said I was just saying that so Mom would let me keep reading the books.

I started reading Jake Konig's books after my dad died in a plane crash caused by terrorists, which is a lot scarier than anything Konig has ever dreamed up. For some reason I feel connected to the characters and the stories. Maybe I like to be frightened about something other than my dad not coming home. Maybe it takes my mind to a different place. All I know is, I can't wait to read the latest book in his Dead End series every time one comes out.

After Mom became a Christian, she wasn't so sure about those books, even though she had once been a friend of Jake's. A lot of parents won't let their kids read them, but Mom said at least I was reading something. She decided I was old enough to understand the difference between what was real and what was made up, and I think she knew the stories helped me in some strange way.

When I heard that Jake Konig was not just coming to our town, but also to our house, I couldn't believe it. I knew he lived somewhere in Colorado, but I never thought I'd get the chance to actually meet him.

The week Mr. Konig was supposed to come I could hardly sit still. I asked Mom why he was coming so many times that she actually growled.

"Bryce, I've told you. I knew him in Chicago when we were both beginners, before either of us had written any books. We were in a writing group together."

"Is he weird like his books?" Ashley said.

Mom smiled. "When I knew him, he was so shy he wouldn't even look girls in the eye."

"Could you tell he was going to be a good writer?" I said.

"We all read each other's stories," she said. "His were pretty strange, about human monsters, puppets that came to life, ghosts, things like that. I knew he'd probably succeed because he always worked so hard at it."

A magazine article said Jake was so rich he owned several houses in different states. His favorite thing to do was ride his huge Harley-Davidson motorcycle.

"But why is he coming here?" Ashley said.

"He's working on a new book and has some questions for me," Mom said. "I've been praying that God will give me the right words to tell him about my faith."

Now there was a thought. I have to admit, it sounded impossible.

CHAPTER 2

❃ Ashley ❃

I didn't see why Bryce was so excited. I mean, Mom's a writer too and her books sell a lot. She's not as famous or rich as Jake Konig, but I'd rather read one of her books any day.

A lot of girls read Jake Konig books. Leigh, our stepsister, who's in high school, reads the adult books. I can always tell when she's starting a new one because she keeps all the lights on at night, and Sam, our stepdad, grumbles as he marches around turning them off.

My friend Hayley reads them too. She loves all that creepy stuff and talks a lot about ghosts and ghouls.

Mom explained that Jake had gotten in touch with her after he read newspaper stories about Bryce and his friend Jeff. They had gone on a long bike ride to raise money for cancer research. Konig had kept up with Mom's career and decided to get reacquainted.

"Won't Sam be jealous?" I said.

Mom grinned and shook her head. "Sam has nothing to worry about from Jake Konig. Anyway, Jake's married too. Sam *will* be jealous of Jake's motorcycle, though."

Mom got us to help straighten up around the house, and she cleaned her office. Then she asked Bryce and me to keep track of our little brother, Dylan. He's four and likes playing with our dogs, Pippin and Frodo. Mauling is more like it. He'll say he's taking them for a walk and then drag the poor things around on their leashes until their tongues hang out.

The day Jake Konig was supposed to arrive, I was outside watching Dylan try to get Frodo up the slide so he could see him fly down. Frodo is a Yorkie that needs a haircut. The wind howled as Frodo stood at the top of the slide with his fur flying. He faced the red rock formation behind our house and stared, like he was looking for another country beyond his electric fence. Pippin, our little white dog, sat in the sand at the edge of the swing set and looked like he was laughing.

The phone rang inside, and a few minutes later I heard Bryce yell, "No! Why?"

I grabbed Dylan and ran inside.

Mom was hanging up the phone as we walked in.

Bryce looked like someone had just torn the cover off one of his favorite books. "Jake's not coming." He took Dylan back outside and let the door slam.

"What?" I said.

Mom pursed her lips. "That was his wife. Jake's disappeared."

CHAPTER 3

☻ *Bryce* ☻

I admit it. At first I thought it was a lame excuse to not come to our house. But over the next few days *The Gazette* from Colorado Springs was full of stories about Jake Konig's disappearance.

It was as eerie as one of his books. He had told his wife and son he was riding his cycle into Shadow Falls to have lunch at his favorite restaurant. The restaurant owner said Jake had come for lunch and left, but no one had seen him or his motorcycle since.

Actually, it reminded me of one of Konig's books, and the newspaper story mentioned that too. In *Cycles*, a teenager rides into the Rocky Mountains on a sunny day. Konig caught the feel of Colorado with every word, painting a picture that made you feel the sun warming the kid as he rode through aspen groves and past huge rock formations.

The farther into the mountains the kid rode, the more mysterious things became. He started seeing weird-looking people in the woods, but when he stopped, they disappeared. He turned back, but the road just led farther and farther from civilization.

Finally, as it was getting dark, the guy drove toward lights in the distance. It turns out he came upon space aliens, and all that was ever found was the guy's motorcycle at the bottom of a ravine.

The Gazette reported that Jake and his wife hadn't been getting along. It also said the police had searched a canyon under the Royal Gorge Bridge, among many other places.

A few days later, *USA Today* ran a story headlined "What Happened to Jake Konig?" It gave even more details of his life but no answers. It also showed pictures of him playing with his son, a few of him and his wife, and some that were supposed to look scary with him in weird clothes, but in every one of them he was smiling. The photographer said he tried to get Jake to look grim and threatening, but he couldn't hold the pose. The photographer finally covered Jake's mouth and nose with his leather jacket and showed just his eyes—glowing. Ashley said the picture creeped her out.

CHAPTER 4

❀ Ashley ❀

The phone call that changed our lives came two weeks after Jake Konig went missing. Mom hung up and asked us to join her and Sam and Leigh in the living room.

She paced like an anxious cat. "That was Jake's editor in New York. I worked with her on a project a few years ago. She wants me to go to Shadow Falls to look at Jake Konig's latest manuscript."

"Cool!" Bryce said. "Can I read it?"

"Look at it for what?" I said.

"To maybe help finish it."

I couldn't believe it. "Why, Mom? You don't like scaring people."

"This would be strictly a ghostwriting job."

"Ghostwriting?" Bryce said.

"It's where I would do the work, but my name wouldn't appear on the book. I would take Jake's first draft, use his notes and the editor's suggestions, and make a book of it."

I stood. "I can't believe you're even considering it, Mom. It's bound to have bad stuff in it. Blood and guts. Killings. That's not what you write."

Mom sat and folded her hands in her lap. "I knew Jake was going to ask for help. That's why he was coming here."

"But, Mom—"

She held up a hand. "Something was going on with him. He asked me to help because there are many spiritual things in the book. He said he wanted to make sure he got it right."

Sam frowned. "I hope you're not doing this for the money, Kathryn. Things are tight right now, but—"

"They are?" I said. "We don't have any money?"

"Business has been slow, and your mother's royalty checks don't come for another few months."

"Does that mean we won't be able to go on vacation?" Bryce said.

"I shouldn't have said anything," Sam said. "We'll be fine."

I wondered if we might have to sell our ATVs. Or the house.

"I was going to suggest you and Bryce go with me to Shadow Falls," Mom said. "But Sam has some flights next week, and I couldn't take Dylan. . . ."

"I'll watch him," Leigh said. "I need money for a car anyway, and I can't find work."

Mom nodded. "You'd have to get up with him every day. That means before seven."

Leigh gave Mom a look. "I can do it."

Bryce said, "Why do they want you to do this, Mom? Do they think he's dead?"

"They don't know, but for some reason they think he might be. They're excited about this book, and they're afraid it could be years before they find him."

Bryce looked like someone had punched him in the stomach. Maybe he didn't think Mom could write Jake Konig's books the way he liked them.

"You're writing Christian stuff now, Mom," I said. "Won't you be . . . ?" I couldn't think of the word.

"Selling out?" Leigh said.

Mom shifted on the couch. Like Bryce and me, Mom hasn't been a Christian that long. I could tell she was struggling. We often talked about how much we wanted Sam and Leigh to become believers.

"I don't want to sell out," Mom said, "and I don't want to let people down, especially you guys. But something about this feels like an opportunity."

"You're not going to change his book into something religious, are you?" Leigh said.

Mom smiled. "Would you read it if I did?"

CHAPTER 5

⚈ *Bryce* ⚈

Mom talked to our pastor, then called the editor. She agreed that Mom could walk away from the job at any point. If she found the manuscript too gory or weird, she didn't have to finish.

The editor insisted that Mom go to Jake Konig's own writing house. He had always been secretive, never e-mailing any of his stories to his publisher because he was afraid someone might steal them. She said he kept one file on his computer and another in a thumb drive he carried around with him on a key chain. That's it.

Armed guards hand carried his pages all the way from Colorado to New York City, as if the manuscript were a precious diamond. It was worth even more than that, if you think about it. The editor said she hadn't even seen this book. Mom would be the first to lay eyes on it.

Ashley and I packed, wondering what we'd find. I was a lot more excited than she was, but when she heard we might get to stay at a bed-and-breakfast inn and hang around town as much as we wanted, I could tell she was warming up to the idea.

A long black limo pulled up to our house at eight the next morning. We could have fit our whole school into the thing. A guy in a suit, who introduced himself as Jake Konig's driver, loaded our luggage into the trunk.

We all said our good-byes, and Dylan started crying, which made it even harder for Mom to leave. She took him inside and got him interested in something else, then slipped out, and we were on our way.

CHAPTER 6

✖ Ashley ✖

We headed north on I-25 and passed the outlet mall in Castle Rock. I love going there just to look in the store windows and eat at the food court. There wasn't much traffic, which was too bad. Secretly I wished people would point at us and wonder who we were in our big limo.

The driver reminded me of the actor who plays the farmer in those Babe movies. ("That'll do, Pig.") Tall, long arms, long nose. His deep-set eyes made him look like a ferret. His name was Gerald, and he had worked for Mr. Konig for seven years.

Bryce sat reading one of the Dead End books he'd already read twice. When he tilted it down, the 3-D picture on the cover changed from a kid walking toward a graveyard to a screaming face. I wished Bryce wouldn't read that stuff, but I wasn't about to order him around just because I'm older (by 57 seconds).

Mom was quiet. She stared out the window with her arms folded. We passed the exit for Red Rocks Amphitheater, where singers and bands perform outside. A lot of people get it mixed up with our town.

After skirting the city of Denver, Gerald turned onto a road that led through Boulder, where the University of Colorado is. I put on earphones and switched on the little TV. It was hooked to a satellite, so I flipped through about a million channels until I saw a news report that had Jake Konig's picture on a screen behind the anchor.

". . . Search teams finished combing his secluded estate outside Shadow Falls yesterday, and authorities ask anyone with information to come forward."

The broadcast cut to a shot of the house, which looked like one of those scary mansions in horror movies, and people in yellow jackets walking along a wooded hillside.

When I noticed Gerald looking at me in the rearview mirror, he turned his eyes back to the road.

CHAPTER 7

☺ *Bryce* ☺

I was getting to the best part of *Grave Screams* as we rode into the mountains. The main character is a kid about my age whose parents die in a freak accident. He's left to take care of his little sister, but things keep making it harder for him. He has grown suspicious of her, wondering if she has some power to hurt people when she gets angry.

The road wound through mountain lakes and summer cottages, and soon we were near Rocky Mountain National Park. Sam once drove us all the way through it, and we had our picture taken at Bear Lake with a 12,000-foot peak behind us.

We passed through small towns gearing up for the Fourth of July. Flags flew from every store and gas station. Shadow Falls came up quickly, and Ashley's eyes lit up at the gift shops. I saw a mom-and-pop video store—no Blockbuster here—and a grocery store. A small river ran alongside the town next to a concrete river walk. Parents were out pushing strollers. A green field opened to our right, where kids threw footballs and Frisbees. Beyond the field sat a redbrick library.

"How far is the house, sir?" Ashley said.

Gerald pointed toward the foothills. "About two miles as the crow flies. Feels farther." He also pointed out a cinder-block path beside the road and said we could use one of the Konigs' golf carts to come into town if we wanted.

"Golf cart?" Ashley said, eyes widening. "Cool!"

We passed a white church with a huge steeple. The sign said Shadow Falls Chapel.

"Look way back up in the trees to your right and you'll see The Broken Saber."

It was a sprawling lodge peeking out of the forest on a ridge. I recognized it from the movie poster. Of course I had never seen the film.

"That's where Konig stayed and got the idea for *Corridor of Blood*," I said. "His first adult book."

"Correct," Gerald said. "They've turned it into a bed-and-breakfast. You can actually stay in the room where Mr. Konig wrote the book. They even sell red doorknobs in the gift shop."

"Red doorknobs?" Ashley said.

"You'd have to read the book, young lady," Gerald said.

"Not a chance," Ashley muttered.

"Maybe we could stay there one night," Mom said.

I gave her a thumbs-up, but Ashley sneered and shook her head.

The road narrowed the farther we wound around the mountain. Finally, we turned onto a gated drive where a police car sat. Ivy climbed the sides of stone pillars, and an iron fence ran around the property. Gerald punched a button over his visor, and the gates crept open.

CHAPTER 8

❈ Ashley ❈

The driveway snaked up steeply to the house, which looked like a castle. Pine trees crowded the way and blocked the sun. The house and land looked like they had spent the last hundred years in the dark. I shuddered.

Gerald parked outside the garage, and the main house loomed above us. Stairs led to the front, but he said we should unload our suitcases and take the golf cart to the writing house. He gave us the security code for the front door and explained to Mom how to get into Jake's computer upstairs.

He looked at his watch. "Mrs. Konig will host you for lunch here at the main house at 12:45. Ring the bell at the back door at that time, please."

The oversized golf cart held four people, plus luggage. Bryce insisted on driving, and we lurched along a small paved road that wound up the hill. A metal railing ran beside the cart path.

Though I didn't think it was possible, the farther back we went, the darker it became. Huge boulders lined the cart path like moss-covered sentries. Suddenly it felt like we were going straight up, and Mom grabbed the handle cut into the plastic roof to steady herself.

The main house faded from sight, but not before I saw someone watching us from a window.

CHAPTER 9

◐ *Bryce* ◑

The writing house was built into the side of the rocky hill and had a killer view of the valley and the waterfall. Trees actually grew from the roof, and it looked like an animal had burrowed above the house.

While Mom headed upstairs, Ashley and I lugged our stuff inside. Curtains covered the windows. It was as if the wood and walls were light starved. We found mostly hardwood floors, except for two bedrooms, which had thick carpet. Downstairs were two more bedrooms and a recreation area with plasma TV, hot tub, dartboard, stuff like that. Everything smelled new, like the place had just been cleaned.

I guessed Jake Konig spent most of his time here and not at the main house down the hill.

We climbed the stairs to the writing loft and found the walls filled with pictures. In the corners stood statues of werewolves, vampires, and monsters of every sort. Jake's framed book covers lined one entire wall. Awards and certificates and framed letters from famous people hung everywhere around the room.

When Mom opened the front shutters, the view made us gasp.

"I'm going to have trouble getting any writing done here," she said. "I'll want to spend the whole day staring out." Mom looked at her watch. "We'd better get unpacked and down to lunch before I try to get into Jake's computer."

"Do we have to go to lunch with you?" I said.

She nodded. "I want you to meet Mrs. Konig so she'll know who you are. Maybe you can meet her son."

Ashley studied a gargoyle. "If he's anything like his dad, I'm not sure I want to."

CHAPTER 10

❀ Ashley ❀

It was my turn to drive the golf cart, but it was a lot scarier going down than coming up. We didn't even need power. I just coasted and rode the brake. Mom held on to the roof handle again and let out a big sigh when we pulled up behind the main house.

A woman dressed in a black uniform answered the door and introduced herself as the maid, Caroline. She had a kind face. "Mrs. Konig will see you in the dining room shortly."

We walked through the kitchen, which sparkled with the latest appliances. The refrigerator was built into the wall and looked twice the size of ours. In the dining room five place settings were neatly arranged at the table.

"It's like that fancy restaurant in the Springs," Bryce whispered. "I won't know which fork to use."

Mom said not to worry. "Start on the outside and work your way in. Or just watch me."

When Mrs. Konig walked in, we all stood. She wasn't pretty like Mom, but she was trim and wore crisp, pleated pants with a silk shirt and a purple scarf. Her hair was short, and she had piercing blue eyes.

"Lorie Konig," she said, offering her hand to my mom.

"I'm so sorry about what's happened," Mom said. "This must be terribly stressful for you."

Mrs. Konig pressed her lips together. "Frankly, I don't know what I think about your working on Jake's book, but that's not your problem. Thank you for coming."

Mom introduced us and we sat. I wondered about the extra place setting next to Bryce.

Caroline served a salad that had little bits of almonds and tangerines and a vinaigrette dressing.

Bryce studied Mrs. Konig before he picked up his little fork.

Mom asked if there was any news on Jake's whereabouts, but Lorie said, "I'd rather not talk about it. But no, there is nothing new."

"How much do you know about his new novel?" Mom said.

Mrs. Konig sipped water from a crystal goblet and pushed her salad away. Her face looked tight. "Jake never talked about his stories while he was working. Not even to me. He thought it was bad luck. I understand he called you."

Mom nodded. "I came because he had asked for my input before he disappeared." She paused as soup was served. Bryce watched the two women like a hawk and picked up his soup spoon only after they did. "I was not aware, however, that you had a problem with my involvement."

Mrs. Konig narrowed her eyes. "I didn't say I had a problem with it. I said I wasn't sure what I thought."

"Had you and Jake discussed it?"

She forced a wry smile. "No. Sounds like you haven't read the tabloids. Jake and I were headed for divorce, if you believe them."

"I'm sorry. If you'd rather not talk about this—"

"I don't mind. The truth is, I still love him. But we've grown apart. You could say that success has changed us."

"How so?" I said.

She seemed startled I'd even talk, especially about her marriage.

Mom gave me a stern look. "Ashley!"

"It's all right," Mrs. Konig said. "The whole world seems to be in our business. When you have as much as we do, as many homes and *things*—" she drew quotation marks with her fingers—"you lose something. In the early years when Jake was struggling, we were working toward a common goal, trying to survive. Now he has his work, his books, movies, television shows, and I have this." She waved at the cavernous room. "And Clancy, of course. Hello, dear."

Clancy, tall and lanky, had longer hair than his mother, an earring, and the same piercing blue eyes. When he looked at me I felt my face turn red.

CHAPTER 11

☺ *Bryce* ☺

Ashley went all googly-eyed. Clancy looked at least two years older than us, and I could tell by his walk that he was an athlete. When we shook hands, I noticed he had calluses.

He kissed his mother on the cheek and apologized for being late. When the chicken with fancy green beans and brown sauce came, he asked Ashley and me about ourselves. I told him everything, and Ashley just sat there nodding and smiling.

"Why don't you show them around town?" Mrs. Konig said.

Clancy rolled his eyes, like he'd rather have his toenails pulled out. He wadded his napkin and put it on his half-finished plate. We followed him outside.

I sat next to him in the front seat of the golf cart, with Mom and Ashley in the back. We dropped Mom off at the writing house, and he jumped out to open the front door for her.

He followed the cinder-block path along the road toward town and showed me a couple of things about the cart—the energy gauge and how to recharge the battery, as if I couldn't figure it out on my own. Ashley gazed at the back of his head like he was some gift from God.

When we got close to town, I said, "You pretty upset about your dad?"

"Me?" Clancy scoffed. "Life's easier without him. He doesn't yell at us for no reason or pull one of his loony acts."

"Loony acts?" Ashley said.

"Yeah, where he runs through the house screaming at us or thinks his characters are coming to get him."

"Sounds scary," Ashley said.

"Mom asked him to move out when he was writing, which means always. He works morning to night. He's obsessed."

"Where do you think he is?" I said.

Clancy shrugged. "Those people might know." He pointed toward the white church with the steeple. "That's where the Holy Rollers go. They protest every time a new book comes out. At least, one guy does. He always shows up at the end of our driveway."

"You think they did something to him?" Ashley said.

"I don't know. He could have run off. He'd been threatening that for a long time. Maybe it was Gerald. He and dad argued a lot."

CHAPTER 12

❀ Ashley ❀

Clancy drove a little fast down hills, but the wind blew his hair toward me, and I couldn't help noticing how strong his face looked. His smile made my knees weak.

I tried to think of something to say, but all I could come up with was, "How long have you lived here?"

"About four years. We still have a couple of houses—California and Chicago—but most of the time we live here."

Clancy said "a couple of houses" like they were gum balls or skateboards. I couldn't imagine having that much money.

He stopped across the road from The Broken Saber. "See that

window?" he said, pointing. "That's where my dad says he saw the ghost. Talked with it."

"The ghost told him a story?" Bryce said.

"Maybe it was a dream. Or maybe Dad made the whole thing up, but he says he met with the thing three nights in a row and stayed up the whole time just writing it down."

"I can't imagine writing three straight nights," Bryce said.

Clancy nodded toward the building. "That spooky place changed my family's life. It's a wonder Dad didn't buy it."

Clancy drove into town and showed us where to park when we were renting a movie or going to the grocery store. Several store workers stared at us.

"Don't mind them," Clancy said. "Half this town lives off the tourists who come here because of my dad. The other half wishes we'd all go away."

Clancy showed us the river walk, pointed out the ski slopes, and walked us into a little bookstore with wood floors and walls that smelled really old. "My dad signs books in here now and then. Says it keeps him in touch with his readers."

The woman behind the counter perked up. "And who do you have with you today, Clancy?"

He introduced us and we moseyed around. I looked for something for Dylan but could find only expensive pop-up books. I spotted a key chain with Jake Konig's name on it that would be perfect for Leigh.

"You go to school around here?" I said.

"Nah," Clancy said. "I go to boarding school in California."

"How often do you come home?"

"Thanksgiving, Christmas, spring break."

"Must get lonely."

He shrugged. "You get used to it. Dad said he'd fly me home every month if my grades were good enough."

"Going back in the fall?" Bryce said.

"Depends on what happens. I'll be a sophomore."

"So you're 14?" I said.

"Just turned 15."

CHAPTER 13

⊙ *Bryce* ⊙

Clancy showed us the best places to eat, including the diner his dad visited for coffee each morning. I could tell Ashley was interested in Clancy, and not because we're twins and I know everything in her head. That's a myth, anyway. I could tell by how quiet she was, and then she'd laugh at something he said like it was the funniest thing on earth. To be honest, Clancy was getting on my nerves, and Ashley wasn't helping things.

When she ducked into a gift shop, Clancy asked me if she had a boyfriend.

I had to smile. "Not really." I started telling him about Skeeter

Messler, a kid in our class who had it bad for her, but Ashley wasn't interested.

Clancy seemed distracted and kept looking away.

Ashley came out smiling. She'd found a park-ranger Jeep for Dylan that lit up and said, "Please don't feed the bears."

Clancy offered to buy us ice-cream cones, and Ashley giggled. I couldn't wait to get back to the Konig place to tell her to knock it off.

As we came out of the ice-cream shop, Clancy stopped and almost dropped his cone. "Uh-oh."

A man in corduroy pants turned from the golf cart and glared at us.

"Hank Clashman," Clancy whispered. "One of the religious crazies."

CHAPTER 14

✖ Ashley ✖

Clashman looked like the angriest human on the planet. He had a goatee and eyes that flashed like fire.

"They find your old man yet, Konig?"

Clancy pushed his way past Clashman and got into the golf cart. He motioned for Bryce and me to join him.

"Publicity stunt," Clashman spat. "He's hiding, milking more money from his godless books. And if you know where he is, you're part of the plan!"

We climbed in, and Clancy tore out of the lot. The cart would go only so fast, though, and we could still hear Clashman yelling as we rolled away.

"What's his problem?" Bryce said.

"Religious wacko. Dad says he follows him all over the place. Christians are nuts."

I wanted to say that we were Christians and we weren't wackos. We didn't yell at people on the street. How would Clancy ever see that Jesus loved him if so-called Christians acted like that?

I told myself to wait for the right chance to talk with Clancy, but I couldn't help feeling Bryce and I were hiding our lights under a basket.

CHAPTER 15

◐ *Bryce* ◑

Mom was working in the loft when we got home. We didn't want to interrupt, but Ashley and I agreed we had to tell her what had happened.

Mom was in the big, cushy chair by the computer, and Ashley and I sat on the leather couch. She opened a little refrigerator built into the wall and offered us soft drinks. Jake must have had a thing for Diet Coke with Lime, because there were a thousand bottles.

"Coming here might not have been the best idea," she said.

"For us or you?" I said.

"Both. If you're being threatened by a protestor and Clancy is trashing your faith . . ."

"We didn't stand up to him," Ashley said. "It was like I betrayed God."

Mom shook her head. "You'll get another chance."

"Why has this been a bad idea for you?" I said.

She sighed. "This place and Jake's story are getting to me. It's about a guy in prison."

"Bad language?" Ashley said.

"Actually it's pretty clean so far. But all these statues and pictures keep me thinking somebody is going to sneak up behind me. Plus, it's like Jake is trying to tell me something. Maybe there's a hidden meaning. Good stories are supposed to work like that, but this is different. The main character seems so much like Jake, and he's in such a struggle. I wish he were here. . . ."

"Do *you* think Jake's disappearance was a publicity stunt?" I said.

She raised her eyebrows. "I don't think so. Doesn't sound like him. If he was going to disappear just for show, he would have left his motorcycle. If there's one thing Jake loved, it was that bike. He took it everywhere and hated cars. He was even going to ride it to our house. But it disappeared when he did."

"If he drove to Timbuktu or somewhere, that's where it would be," I said.

"But the police and people all over the country have been on the lookout for him and have come up with nothing. And . . ." Mom ran her hand across the desk and hesitated.

"What?" Ashley said.

"I don't want to scare you."

"Tell us, Mom."

"In one of his books a character goes crazy and thinks he's a bird. He hops on his motorcycle—the same kind Jake rides—and he drives off the Royal Gorge Bridge."

"Is that why the police checked there?" Ashley said.

Mom nodded. "I don't know that you can actually drive off the bridge, but his editor said Jake has been acting weird lately, stranger than normal. And there's other stuff, notes that trouble me."

"Notes?" I said.

"He writes in the margins. Several times I've seen the initials *PS*. 'PS thinks this' or 'PS said that.' 'Met with PS today,' that sort of thing."

I smiled. "What if PS works for the FBI and sent his ID via UPS to the CIA?"

They didn't laugh.

Ashley scratched her head. "You think PS could be the one who made him disappear?"

"No idea. But something else bothers me. What if PS is someone Jake made up? Or conjured up?"

"You mean like a demon?" I said.

She stared at the floor. "I wouldn't put it past him."

"You're right, Mom," Ashley said. "This is scary."

"Maybe Mrs. Konig or Clancy knows," I said.

"They haven't spent much time with him for months," Mom said. "He stayed here writing and only came out to go to some diner."

"We saw it," Ashley said. "We should go there and ask around. See if anybody knows—" Ashley stopped midsentence, staring at Mom.

"What is it, Ash?" Mom said.

Ashley's face went white, and she pointed to the computer monitor.

Words moved across the screen as if they were actually being typed as we watched.

Is anybody there? I need your help. Please.

CHAPTER 16

✖ Ashley ✖

I couldn't breathe, couldn't move. The message continued.

If you can read this, get help right away. I'm being h—

As quickly as the message had come, it stopped.

I didn't want to spend another minute in that house. Everywhere I looked some creepy statue or gargoyle seemed to be grinning at me. I stood and stared out the window into the valley, trying to keep from screaming.

"We should get out of here," Mom said.

"Wait," Bryce said in a surprisingly firm voice. "That had to be Jake Konig trying to send us a message."

"From the dead?" I yelled. "Let's go. Now!"

"Stop it, Ash. Not from the dead. It looked like it was being typed right then."

"More likely it was programmed into the computer," Mom said. "Like a screen saver." She slid in front of the monitor and tried to bring the message back. When that didn't work she typed out the message so we could remember it.

"We should call the police," I said, shaking.

Mom looked at me like she was afraid I was going to lose it right there.

"Somebody's trying to mess with our minds," Bryce said.

We were staring at the computer screen when it suddenly went blank.

Mom scooted back and raised her hands to show she wasn't touching the keyboard.

The screen faded to gray with a black border, then flashed two gigantic words:

GET OUT!

CHAPTER 17

☺ *Bryce* ☺

I didn't blame Ashley for screaming, but it felt like I'd never hear out of my right ear again. Mom jumped from the chair, and we raced downstairs and out the front door.

The whole thing felt like a scary movie, the kind I like. But I didn't want to be part of one.

We ran past the golf cart and down the hill to the main house. Someone was staring out a back window. It looked like Gerald, and I would have sworn he was smiling.

We stood there panting like dogs when Mrs. Konig rushed out. Mom explained what had happened, and Mrs. Konig invited us in, hollering down the stairs for Clancy. I could tell Ashley was trying to calm herself as Clancy appeared.

He smirked when he heard what had happened. "Dad programmed bizarre stuff to just go off on his machine to keep him on his toes while he was writing."

"But why would he program a message asking for help?" I said.

Clancy shrugged. "I'll take a look at it if you want."

"Maybe we should tell the police," Mom said.

"No," Mrs. Konig said quickly. She took a breath and closed her eyes. "They were traipsing all over the property the other day, and I don't want them back."

I couldn't imagine not wanting the police to investigate everything that might have to do with your husband's disappearance, and it must have showed on my face.

"I hope you understand," Mrs. Konig said. "I'll have Gerald look at the computer."

Clancy shot his mother a look. "Yeah, and you can forget that I just offered to do the same."

"Now, dear, you know Gerald is in charge of—"

Clancy waved her off and headed back downstairs.

Mom said, "I'd appreciate any help. We're not up for more excitement."

"Would you rather stay here with us?"

I looked at Mom and shook my head. No way we would get to the bottom of this if we stayed with Clancy and his mother. Ashley looked like she was about to jump out of her skin.

"No thanks," Mom said. "If it checks out, we'll stay there tonight."

"Fine, but do come back and join us for dinner. I'll tell Caroline." She moved to the door that led downstairs. "Clancy, honey, would you like to play tennis with Bryce and Ashley?"

There was a long pause.

"Clancy?"

"Fine," he whined.

That was the last thing I wanted to do. I wanted to be there when Gerald checked the computer. "You two go ahead," I told Ashley.

CHAPTER 18

✖ Ashley ✖

I was relieved to stay away from that writing house, and it felt good to be outside. Okay, I also loved the idea of a little alone time with Clancy. And he seemed to want to play, even though he'd acted weird when his mom suggested it. He grabbed two rackets and a new can of balls from an outbuilding. I love the *pfft* of the air whooshing out of a tennis-ball can and the smell of the rubber.

"I didn't even know you had a tennis court," I said.

"It's hidden back here. Mom had it built after we moved in. We might have to sweep the pine needles off, but it's nice."

As we walked to the court I realized how dead everything seemed at the house. No music. No little kids. No pets. Not even bird feeders. The only animals were squirrels scurrying along the hillside, and they were just searching for food. The whole place felt sterilized, like a hospital. The writing house was disturbing, but at least it was interesting.

The court was around the hill and overlooked another side of the mountain. It seemed anywhere you turned held a spectacular view.

A black chain-link fence ran around the green-and-red court. A huge green backboard hung on the fence with a white line painted as high as the net.

After we swept the court, Clancy tossed me a ball and stuffed the other two in his pocket. "You play much?"

"Bryce and I play doubles a lot."

He settled into position, much too deep for my game, and said, "Serve it up."

I was nervous but hit the serve pretty deep to his backhand. One swing was all I needed to see that Clancy was in another league. He hit the ball squarely in the center of his racket with a *thwop*. That's one of the best sounds in the world. He seemed to play without effort, gliding to retrieve my missed hits. I know you're supposed to watch the ball and everything, but it was hard to concentrate.

"You're really good," I said.

He smiled. "Mom hired a pro to teach me. There aren't that many people to play with around here, so I spend a lot of time hitting against the backboard."

We played a set, and I could tell Clancy was taking it easy on me. His serve was amazing. He tossed the ball perfectly and hit it with such topspin that it jumped after hitting my side. When I hit it, the ball flew in the air—an unintentional lob. He lightened up on his serve, but each time he came to the net he was able to put my return away easily.

The score was 4-0 with him serving at 30-love when I said, "You've been holding back. Hit a first serve at full speed and see if I can return it."

"You sure?" he said, smiling.

I nodded.

He tossed the ball, left his feet, swung with a grunt, and by the time his feet hit the ground the ball had skipped through the service box, flashed past me, and stuck in the fence behind me. I hadn't even had time to raise my racket, let alone swing.

I worked the ball loose from the fence, and we switched sides. I got a few points but not many.

There was a drink dispenser in the little building beside the court, and we sat on a bench with cans of lemonade. "You're not bad," Clancy said.

"I'm better at doubles. You'd get a lot more competition with Bryce."

He shrugged. "I wouldn't have as much fun."

I'd forgotten about the eerie computer message already. But I'd also forgotten to bring up the faith thing.

CHAPTER 19

☺ *Bryce* ☺

I told Mom I thought she was right about telling the police.

Mom nodded. "We'll keep a record and get it to the police after we leave, even if Lorie doesn't want us to."

When Gerald showed up he seemed aloof and bored. He went straight to the computer and tapped a few keys, pulling up a program.

"What's this?" I said, determined to loosen him up.

He sniffed. "Just random phrases and sentences Mr. Konig uses to shock himself and keep his mind alert. They pop up on the screen unexpectedly."

Gerald sat back from the monitor and let us see. The phrases and sentences were odd—some didn't make sense, and others looked like they were in a different language.

Mom studied the screen. "I suppose I can see how these might give him some inspiration. I have quotes from different writers that scroll across as a screen saver. But I don't see anything close to what we saw."

"Are you sure you didn't hit any keys?" Gerald said. "Maybe you called up something else he was working on?"

"We weren't even close to the keyboard," I said.

Gerald grinned. "Well, there you have it. That's the answer."

I looked at Mom. "What?"

"It had to be a ghost," he said.

Mom cocked her head. "Very funny. Sir, if I may ask, what do you remember about the day Jake disappeared?"

"What are you driving at?"

"Where were you when you heard?"

Gerald leaned back and looked at the ceiling. "Down at the gate, waiting for a contractor due for some paving work. Mr. Konig left before noon for the diner and said he'd be back at two. When he wasn't back by three and I couldn't raise him on his cell phone, I called the place. He'd been there and gone. That morning was the last I saw of him."

"Did he leave his computer on?" Mom said. "Was he working on something he was going to come back to?"

Gerald seemed to consider Mom, as if she had no business asking such questions. "Mr. Konig always leaves his computer running. He turns off the monitor, and he protects his work with a password, but the machine's on 24/7."

"It was off when we got here," Mom said. "I had to use the password you gave me to get into the system."

"Right. I did that. Can't be too careful."

CHAPTER 20

❀ Ashley ❀

"We have a theater downstairs in the house," Clancy said. "You should come over and watch something."

"I'd love it. Bryce too. But we wouldn't be able to watch any of your dad's movies."

He turned and stared at me. "What? Why?"

"We rarely even watch PG-13s."

"You've got to be kidding."

I felt my face turning red again. I didn't want to seem so sheltered, especially to Clancy.

"Well," he said, "I don't like my dad's movies anyway. We might have *Bambi* or *Snow White* down there somewhere."

"Come on!"

"Sorry," he said, leaning over and nudging me with his shoulder. "Couldn't resist."

I was in heaven. So why couldn't I talk about God?

"If your mom is so uptight about movies, why's she working on my dad's book?"

I shrugged. "He asked her to look it over. I think she feels it's the least she can do now. His publisher came up with the idea of her finishing it. She talked it over with our pastor—"

"Pastor? Don't tell me—"

"Yeah." I giggled. "Guess we're some of those crazies, huh?"

CHAPTER 21

☺ *Bryce* ☺

Clancy hardly looked at us at dinner, and it wasn't until after we left that Ashley told me he probably thought we were religious nuts.

"But he asked us to come and watch a movie sometime," I said.

"That was before I told him we don't watch many PG-13s."

When the sun crested the hill behind the writing house, shadows fell across the front. No wonder they called it Shadow Falls. It looked like a huge bird had covered the sun with its wings.

Mom and Ashley seemed okay with staying in the writing house, maybe because they'd be sleeping in the same room. I was sleeping alone, and I wasn't about to ask Mom if I could sleep on the floor in their room.

I helped Mom figure out the printer. Jake had every machine in the writing room hooked to a battery backup. Even the coffeemaker. Mom printed a couple of chapters while Ashley and I watched TV.

It's never easy for us to agree on what to watch. I like baseball, but she likes gymnastics. I like scary movies, but she likes movies that make her cry. (She would deny this.)

We agreed on a TV series produced by Jake Konig's company, which was fine at first. But the story got scarier and scarier. Faces behind doors. Visions and dreams of death. On my way to the kitchen during a commercial, I didn't even look out the windows, not wanting to see anything that looked like a human face.

Mom had a fire going in the fireplace. The lamp was on above her, and she had her reading glasses pulled down on her nose.

The phone rang, making her jump. I slowed as she picked it up.

"Oh no," she said.

CHAPTER 22

❀ Ashley ❀

Whatever was wrong, it wouldn't have bothered me a bit if we had headed back home at that very moment. I was tired of thinking about Jake Konig and what might have become of him. I didn't want to leave Clancy, but it was clear he was done with us.

Done with me.

"Have you looked outside?" Mom said.

I stood, muting the TV. *Dylan?*

"What is it?" Bryce said.

Mom covered the phone. "Leigh can't find Dylan's Blue's Clues blanket and he's . . ." She held out the phone, and we both heard Dylan screaming his head off.

We couldn't help laughing. First, it was a relief to know Dylan hadn't wandered off to Kansas, but it was also funny because Leigh had to deal with it.

I motioned for the phone. "Leigh, let me talk with him."

"It's not going to do any good," she sobbed. "I swear he won't shut up."

"Just tell him I want to talk with him."

Leigh tried three times to tell him, but he was crying too hard. I imagined his little face, all puffy and red, tears streaming, stuff coming out of his nose.

"Dylan, listen to me! It's Ashley!"

He stopped crying, then snorted so loud I couldn't keep from laughing. That sent him into another wailing spasm.

"Dylan! I bought something for you today!"

Finally he quieted.

"I was at this little store, thinking of you, and you know what?" I waited.

Another snort. "What?"

"It's a special car that lights up and talks. Would you like that?"

"Yeah."

"Well, I have it here, and I'm going to give it to you as soon as I get there, okay?"

No answer. Then, "When are you coming home?"

"It won't be long," I said, realizing that the goal was to get him to stop crying, not to give an exact date. "Now you listen to Leigh and go to sleep, and before you know it—"

"I want the car that talks," Dylan said. He was close to tears again.

"Tell him we'll mail it to him tomorrow," Mom said.

"Dylan? If you calm down and Leigh says you behaved, we'll mail it to you and you'll get it even sooner. But you have to stop crying and go to sleep, okay?"

A long pause. Then, weakly, "Okay. Bye."

We could only imagine what Leigh had gone through in the last hour.

Bryce and I decided we didn't want to watch the Konig show anymore, and I let him turn on the Cubs game. They were playing in San Francisco and a Giant was circling the bases. The camera cut to a shot of a baseball bobbing in the water of McCovey Cove beyond the right-field wall, and Bryce groaned.

I looked through a stack of DVDs under the TV. Every one had the word *dead, corpse,* or *blood* in the title.

I found another disc lying on the DVD player, and it stood out because of a handwritten title on the spine in black magic marker: "Gassy Pastor." When I opened it there was no DVD inside, but a piece of paper fell out. A note dated a couple of weeks earlier was scrawled in red.

Dear Jake,

I've enjoyed our conversations. Here's the DVD I told you about. Not all of "us" have such a small sense of humor.

TS

I finally found the DVD in the player, and the Cubs were already so far behind that Bryce said he wanted to see it too. It showed a preacher asking a TV audience for money, but whoever produced the disc had dubbed in noises that made it sound like the guy had been eating beans for three weeks before the show.

I couldn't stop laughing, and Bryce was on the floor, banging his hand on the carpet, begging me to stop it so he could breathe. Mom usually doesn't like stuff like that, but even she was laughing.

When we finally stopped, Bryce held up a hand. "Who do you think gave that to Jake?"

Mom shrugged. "TS, PS. I'm confused."

CHAPTER 23

◑ *Bryce* ◑

Going into that bedroom alone was hard. First I closed the curtains. I didn't even want to think about what might be outside.

Then I switched on the TV to watch the rest of the Cubs game. I root for the Rockies, but the Cubs are my team because my real dad used to take me to games at Wrigley. It feels like betraying him to root for another team, so I also follow Chicago long-distance.

When the game was delayed by rain, I switched to a special program called "The Last Words of Jake Konig?" I immediately hit the Record button.

The host showed Konig riding his motorcycle and signing for

hundreds of fans, clips of scary movies, and a brief history of his career. He followed with an interview conducted only a few weeks before.

Konig laughed about his title as The Scariest Man on Earth. "I was a frightened kid scared of my own shadow. I turned that fear into something that worked for me. I've made a lot of money making people scream and not want to get in their automobiles."

The interviewer shifted gears. "Let's talk about Jake Konig, the husband and father—the person. Any regrets as father?"

Jake bit his lip. "Not sure I can pick just one. I've recently realized that I haven't spent as much time with my son as I should have. I've been too busy."

Later the interviewer said, "A lot of people think you're Satan with Microsoft Word. That your stories come straight from the devil."

Konig smiled. "I don't need the devil to give me stories. They come from my own experiences and fears. My stories have a lot more to do with God than the devil."

"You believe in God?"

"Maybe not the way some people want me to believe, but you can't live in a world like ours that has so many evil things going on and not believe in something on the other side, something good. I do believe in good and evil."

A few minutes later Jake leaned forward. "I have friends who try to bring me to the light, so to speak. Some of them have convincing answers to life's questions."

"How does Jake Konig want to be remembered?"

"Well, how I *want* to be remembered and how I *will* be remembered are two different things. I guess I have some time to change that. At least I hope I do."

When the interview clip ended, the host turned to the camera. "Many believe those may have been the last words of Jake Konig. Perhaps the best-selling novelist had less time than he thought."

CHAPTER 24

❀ Ashley ❀

Bryce played the Jake Konig interview for me at breakfast. Mom was already working upstairs.

"Wonder if TS is one of his Christian friends," Bryce said.

"Or PS," I said.

"Maybe they're brothers."

"Or sisters."

"I wonder if there's a way to get into his e-mail," Bryce said, snapping his fingers.

"What?" I said.

He put a finger to his lips. "Wait here." He ran upstairs.

A few minutes later he was back, carrying something. "Couldn't get into his e-mail. We'll have to ask Gerald about that."

I shook my head. "Not that guy . . ."

"Then maybe Clancy," Bryce said.

I rolled my eyes. "I don't think he'll ever talk to us again."

Bryce flipped an envelope to me. "Check this out. I found it on a stack of books by his computer."

It looked like an invitation. Inside was a white card with a picture of a fireplace and a table with cider-filled mugs, cookies and chocolate on a plate, and a bottle of wine.

> *Bring a loved one and spend a frightfully fun weekend with your friends at The Broken Saber. See the very room in this historic inn that gave Jake Konig the inspiration to write Corridor of Blood. Stay in a suite such as the Boo View, Haunted Horseman, Crimson Eyes . . . we'll throw in goodies and a book autographed by the author.*
>   *Earl Rosel, proprietor*

CHAPTER 25

◉ *Bryce* ◉

We needed to talk to this Rosel guy, but I knew Ashley would rather have nothing to do with the case.

"I'll let you drive the cart," I said.

She gave me a look that would have put a wart on a gravestone, but she climbed in behind the wheel.

When we got down to the main house, Ashley hit the brake and the tires squealed. My Cubs hat flew off and landed in the water fountain.

I was fishing it out when Caroline came out the back door. "Sorry," I said. "My sister thinks she's Jeff Gordon."

Caroline didn't smile, and I couldn't tell whether it was because she wasn't a NASCAR fan or because the tires had left black marks on the patio.

"I didn't know the brake was that sensitive," Ashley said.

"Just take it easy, hm?"

"Clancy around?" I said.

"Um, not at the moment. Perhaps you can come back later. Phoning first would be even better."

Ashley glanced at me with a told-you-so look.

"We were wondering about e-mail," I said. "Do you know if my mom will be able to get into any of Jake's messages?"

She shook her head. "He used a different computer for that. Don't know why. Anyway, the authorities confiscated that one."

"Well, thanks. We'll call for Clancy later."

Caroline didn't respond. She just looked down her nose again at the tire marks and walked away.

"She really needs to see the Gassy Pastor," I said.

CHAPTER 26

Ashley

Despite my experience at the Konigs, I liked driving the golf cart. It was almost like driving a car.

The Broken Saber bed-and-breakfast sat on a knoll overlooking the street. Huge white columns rose in front like in those plantation houses from the Civil War.

Bryce had studied it and said it dated to the early 1900s. "It used to be a place for rich people wanting to get away from the city. The guy built it because he had gotten sick a few years earlier and said every time he came to Shadow Falls, he felt better. Presidents have stayed here."

"Looks lonely," I said. There were no cars in the parking lot, and the only movement came from a few horses in a corral at the back of the property. I thought it would be fun to go riding, but Bryce isn't into horses.

I imagined sitting on one of the benches on the porch and watching the waterfall with a date. Maybe Clancy. A sign showed the menu. The prices looked way too expensive for our family, but I figured the Konigs could eat here every day and not blink.

"They have weddings here," Bryce said, pointing to a gazebo partly hidden by a rock wall. "Maybe you and Clancy will have yours here."

"Funny."

Stepping onto the porch gave me a feeling of going back in time. I imagined myself a rich wife, with a long, white dress and puffy sleeves, parasol on my shoulder. But something about the building felt as unnatural as the Konig place. Maybe it was the creaking boards or the way the shadows played off the windows.

Or it could have been the man standing at the side of the porch, watching us.

CHAPTER 27

◎ *Bryce* ◎

Mr. Rosel looked a little like Gerald, tall with a longish nose, but he was older and had less hair, a plain face, and feet too small for his height. He looked at us like we were standing on a sacred grave.

I tried to win him over by cheerily introducing ourselves and asking if this was really the hotel where Jake Konig wrote *Corridor of Blood.*

He took a deep breath, as if it would kill him to tell the story one more time. "Room 213. Konig wrote only children's books up to that point. Coming here changed his career. Now—"

"Do you give tours?" Ashley said.

"When we're not renovating, which we are." He pointed to a sign I hadn't seen that instructed tourists to return in two weeks. "Now if you'll excuse me—"

I pulled out my copy of the invitation I'd found in Jake's office. "Will this still be good then?"

He studied the invitation and snorted. "This is a year old. Prices have gone up since then anyway. Now if you'll—"

"My mom's interested in staying here a night," I said. "Maybe two."

"Great," he said dismissively. "Run along now. . . ."

"We're staying at Jake's," I said, stopping him. "We found this in his writing house."

CHAPTER 28

✖ Ashley ✖

What Bryce said changed us from nuisances to royalty in Mr. Rosel's eyes.

"Well," he said, smiling. I had no idea a man could have that many teeth. "You're really staying at the Konig estate?" He motioned to one of the benches, and we sat. "We have quite a collection of Mr. Konig's books. Are you friends of the family?"

"Sort of," Bryce said. "Our mom's a writer. Before Mr. Konig disappeared . . ."

I shot Bryce a stare, like he was giving away the combination to a secret lock, and he hesitated.

". . . he called her. We're staying there until she finishes her work."

"Really," Mr. Rosel said, stretching the word to syllables. "Has your mother written anything I would know?"

I rattled off a few titles, and he shook his head.

He fell serious, his tone grave. "I can't imagine what that poor woman and her son are going through. Have they heard anything?"

"Not really," I said.

Mr. Rosel sighed. "I hope he's alive. For his sake, of course, but for ours as well. Our business comes from his fans."

"If he's dead, won't people still come?"

He nodded. "Maybe even more will come. I've thought about some kind of memorial, but I certainly hope it doesn't come to that."

"You must be a big fan," Bryce said.

"It's why I bought this place. Mr. Konig captures our fears in such a human way. I hope we haven't read the last of his works."

"What do you think happened to him?" I said.

The morning sun caught his forehead, and he got a far-off look. "No idea. I can still remember hearing his motorcycle pass the day he disappeared. When I hear a loud engine, I think he's come back to us. But in my bones I fear he's gone for good."

CHAPTER 29

☺ *Bryce* ☺

When Mr. Rosel's cell phone went off, it played the theme from Jake Konig's movie *Blood Corridors*. He slipped away to take the call.

"He seems really torn up about Konig," Ashley said.

I wasn't sure what to make of him yet.

Mr. Rosel returned, flipping his phone shut. "Sorry," he said. "Someone looking for a signed first-edition copy of a Konig book."

"Prices are probably going up," I said.

He nodded.

"I'd love to see your library," Ashley said.

"And I'd love to show it to you. Perhaps we can even work out something so your mother can enjoy a stay before we're finished with the renovation." He handed me his card. "Have her call me."

"One more question," I said. "Do the initials *TS* or *PS* mean anything to you?"

Mr. Rosel studied the sky. "Don't think so. Why?"

"Just wondering. Thought it could be somebody around here."

He wiped sweat from his forehead with a handkerchief. "I've lived here only three years. You might ask around."

CHAPTER 30

❀ Ashley ❀

Mom found us in the kitchen having lunch. She looked frazzled. "Jake's a good writer, but this story has my stomach in knots. A guy getting out of prison . . . well, I'm not sure what he's going to do. It feels like those old werewolf movies, where the guy who turns into the wolf wants to live but not hurt anyone."

"But when the werewolf side takes over, he can't control himself," Bryce said.

"Sounds like girls in middle school," I said.

Mom raised her eyebrows. "I got a call from Leigh this morning too. She found Dylan's blanket, but he tossed his Pop-Tarts all over it. Leigh was pretty grossed out."

"One more load of laundry won't kill her," I said.

Bryce told Mom about Mr. Rosel and The Broken Saber. She seemed even more interested in visiting when we described how nice it was.

"Did you get some lunch, Mom?" I said.

"No, I'm saving up for dinner. You two think you could drive me to the diner tonight?"

"Driver!" Bryce yelled.

"Shotgun," I said.

Mom smiled. "And there's a message on the machine for you, Ash."

I punched the button and heard Clancy's voice. "Hi, Ashley. I got a new video and was wondering if you'd want to watch it with me tonight. Kind of an action-comedy thing. Bryce too, if he wants. Call me."

CHAPTER 31

☻ *Bryce* ☻

Trying to keep focused on the Konig case, I shut myself in
my room and read a little of one of Jake's young adult books I hadn't
seen before. *Night of the Tooth Fairy* is about a kid around my age
who had a bratty younger brother. When he got $3 for a tooth, he
put the money back under his pillow with a note asking for more.
That night the older brother was awake when the tooth fairy
showed up and put the brat under a spell for being ungrateful. The
big brother had to go on an odyssey to break the spell.

Reading that scared me. Besides, I was beginning to see that
every Konig story ended with the people the same as they were at

the start. I skipped to the end and read the last chapter. Somehow the kid had defeated the fairy's curse and had his little brother back. But the brat wanted even more money and was just as ungrateful.

At 5:30 Mom and Ashley and I hopped in the golf cart and headed toward town. Mom reminded us not to tell anyone who she was or what she was doing. I didn't admit that I had already told Mr. Rosel too much.

The Shadow Diner was a house that had been converted into an eatery. There were tables throughout and booths around the walls. A waitress carrying dishes said we could seat ourselves. The skin beneath her chin hung like a turkey wattle, and she wore those white shoes nurses wear. I asked her where the Jake Konig booth was.

She stopped and nodded toward a hallway. "Back that way," she said. It was darker in that section and looked like a storage area. There was a pay phone on the wall, along with extra high chairs stacked like old wood. The restrooms were back there too.

A picture of Jake eating at that very booth hung on the wall. He was smiling, his spoon raised over a bowl of chili in some kind of salute. Underneath he had written, "Best grub in the Falls, Jake Konig."

"Is it true he always ate at this booth?" Ashley asked the waitress when she came for our order.

"If we knew he was coming," she said, as if she'd said it 50 times already that day.

Our food came quickly, and we agreed with Jake's view of the "grub." No wonder he kept coming back.

When we finished, the waitress returned in a better mood. On her break she even pulled up a chair and answered our questions. What Jake liked to order. (The barbecue-pork sandwich was his favorite.) If he wrote at the booth. (Never, though she had seen him making notes a few times.) Whether he ate alone or not. (Usually, though his family had been in here. Sometimes he'd bring an out-of-town guest.)

"Did you recognize any of the people he ate with?" I said.

"Nah. Sometimes it would be Hollywood types or publishing people. A writer passing through."

"Do you know if he ever ate with anyone with the initials *TS* or *PS*?" Ashley said.

She scrunched up her face, which made her look like an overused road map. "He introduced them, but I couldn't spare the memory to lodge any names in this brain. We get a lot of people in here, a lot of orders."

"What do you think happened to Jake?" Ashley said.

She looked at her watch, stood, and leaned over the table. Even her lipstick looked wrinkled. She whispered, "That wife of his is meaner'n a snake. She came in here only once and left before she'd taken two bites. Said she'd rather eat at a truck stop. And that boy of theirs, always in trouble. Had to send him away to school, where he only got in more hot water. Wouldn't surprise me if he had something to do with it. Maybe both of them."

CHAPTER 32

✖ Ashley ✖

The waitress shook me up, even though what she said didn't make much sense. If Jake's wife or son had anything to do with his disappearance, what would they still be doing here? With all those houses they own everywhere, it seems like they would want out.

All the way back to the writing house I wondered what kind of trouble Clancy could have gotten into. That would be kind of a tough thing to bring up with him.

He was waiting for us at seven when Bryce and I walked down the cart path to the main house. The mountains were already blocking the sun.

The Konigs' little theater must have cost a fortune. Twenty

leather seats tilted back and had padded foot- and armrests. Big speakers surrounded us. A cabinet held hundreds of DVDs.

"You guys want to help me make some popcorn before we start?" Clancy said.

Bryce rolled his eyes, which was a relief, because I wanted to talk with Clancy alone.

"I'll stay here and look through your movies," Bryce said.

I followed Clancy to the family room, a long walk from the theater. The popcorn machine was totally electronic. Clancy just programmed in that he wanted "Movie Theater Butter," put the ingredients in, and we watched it go to work.

I told Clancy that Bryce had found a copy of his dad's book about the tooth fairy.

"Ugh," he said. "That book. There's a story behind it."

"I'd love to hear it."

"I was eight. Third grade. I pulled my own tooth on my way back from school. I got blood all over my hands and shirt, so when I got home Dad yelled at me and sent me to my room to get cleaned up and change. Maybe he felt bad, because the next morning there were three dollars under my pillow. Of course, I believed it had come from the tooth fairy. I really believed the thing existed. So I wrote a note, something like, 'Could you please give me five dollars next time since there was a lot of blood and it really hurt?'"

I laughed. "What happened?"

"Next morning there was a string taped to the ceiling with a Post-it note hanging right in front of my face. It said, 'Ask for more money and I'll knock the rest of your teeth out.'"

"That's cruel."

"I was scared to death. I never put another tooth under my pillow. So Dad used that idea for one of his stories. In fact, a lot of them came from stuff I was scared about. I asked him to stop, but actual conversations we'd had would wind up in his books."

"Did you feel used?"

The corn had begun popping. "I wished he wasn't my father. I'd find stuff from my e-mails to him in his books. He wrote about my schoolwork, about me—of course not using my name. But if I knew, I figured so did everybody else. There were times I hoped he'd crash his Harley or die in a plane crash."

I flinched, and a lump rose in my throat so fast that I could barely speak. "Oh!" I said, as if I'd been knifed. "Don't say that. Don't even think it."

"You okay? I didn't mean it. I was just telling you how I felt."

"My dad died in a plane crash."

"Oh, man! I'm so sorry. I didn't know. You have to believe I didn't know."

"It's all right."

"No, it's not. I'm such an idiot."

I shook my head, thoroughly embarrassed, but not as embarrassed as Clancy.

The corn popped furiously in the corner, and it looked like we'd have enough for 10 movies. Clancy's story made me suspect him even more, but if he had done something to his father, why would he be telling me this? Was he feeling guilty, or did he just need to talk with someone about his dad?

I wanted to ask him what had happened at school, but I didn't want to ruin my chances of finding out other stuff. I said, "Was your dad going through anything before he disappeared?"

"Like what?"

I took a deep breath. "Talking about spiritual stuff? Thinking about God?"

Clancy's laugh matched the cadence of the popping corn. "My dad getting religious? That's funny. You church types think that's all anybody thinks about."

CHAPTER 33

☺ *Bryce* ☺

The Konig movie collection had *Gone With the Wind* and *Forrest Gump* and everything in between. There were war movies like *Saving Private Ryan* and *We Were Soldiers*, but most of them were dramas.

The popcorn smell from the other room made me remember when our real dad took Ashley and me to the movies. Once, he surprised us by picking us up at school—we didn't know what to think—and taking us to the new Disney movie he knew we were dying to see.

He always got us popcorn and candy, and it made me sad to think

Dylan wouldn't get to do that. That doesn't mean I don't like Sam, but I sure miss my dad.

Clancy and Ashley came back with the best popcorn I've ever tasted, and when he dimmed the lights it felt like we were in an actual theater.

I had seen a trailer for the movie a couple of weeks earlier, and here we were watching it in Clancy's house. He had to have some good friends in the movie business to let him see it before its release.

The story was about two friends who liked the same girl and how one didn't want to hurt the other's feelings and didn't say anything, even though the girl secretly liked him. It was funny and left you with a good feeling.

When Clancy turned up the lights, I started picking up the popcorn I had dropped.

"Don't do that," Clancy said. "That's Caroline's job."

I picked it up anyway. I hate walking over people's trash in a theater, let alone at somebody's house. Anyway, I'm not used to having paid help.

It was almost 10 when we went upstairs. The house was quiet.

"Come back tomorrow and we'll watch something else," Clancy said.

"Sounds fun," Ashley said. "Maybe after church."

"You're going to church?" Clancy said, as if we'd said we were flying to the moon. "Even on vacation?"

"You should come with us," I said.

"No thanks," he said. "Why would I go where people hate me?"

CHAPTER 34

❀ Ashley ❀

I felt bad that Clancy thought people hated him. If it was true, it made me ashamed of Christians who would judge a kid just because they didn't like his father. Or his hair. Or his earring.

On the other hand, maybe the people at church knew more than we did. Maybe they knew what Clancy had done at school.

As soon as we were out the door I was sorry we hadn't driven the golf cart. It was dark, and all I could think of were the statues, paintings, and book covers in Jake's writing room. I imagined he had been attacked by some animal on his way to the main house. That didn't explain his not coming back from lunch or the fact that his motorcycle was also missing, but that's what fear put in my head.

Bryce stopped in the middle of the path. "Did you hear that?"

"Stop it," I said.

What if the animal smells the popcorn butter on us?

"Come on," Bryce whispered. "Let's go."

The path never felt this steep in the daylight. Now it also seemed twice as long. My legs ached.

Bryce held up a hand as something skittered along the cart path. A squirrel? A person?

Some people whistle in the dark. Bryce's friend Jeff told bad jokes when things got hairy. I make up poems when I'm scared.

> *Popcorn, popcorn, yellow and white,*
> *Help me make it home tonight.*
> *Kernels so good, tasty and sweet,*
> *Give us wings for our four feet!*

I grabbed Bryce's shirt and raced for the house.

CHAPTER 35

© Bryce ©

By the time I went to bed, I was still wondering what was making noise outside, but I couldn't make myself look out the window.

In the morning we didn't want everyone knowing we were staying with the Konigs, so instead of letting Gerald drive us to church or even taking the telltale golf cart, Mom called a cab. It took a painfully long time to come, so we were late. The service had already started, and there was no one at the door to greet us or hand us a bulletin. We slipped into one of the back pews.

Everything inside and outside the church was white, except for the oak trim on the doors and edges of the pews. The pulpit was white, the walls were white, even the choir robes were white. It looked like it had snowed inside.

The Colorado and American flags stood behind the choir, along with the Christian flag. The congregation stood and sang from hymnals.

I figured there were maybe 150 people in the service, and most had white hair and wrinkled skin. Many of the men wore suits and ties, which was different from our church. I felt awkward in my jeans. During the offering one of the few kids our age, a girl, sang a solo. I guessed her mother was playing the piano, because they looked alike—except the girl looked like a gust of wind would knock her over, and the mom could barely fit on the piano bench, if you know what I mean.

The pastor preached on God's grace, and you could tell by the way he talked that he wasn't just talking—he knew it. He told of when he was a teenager starting to drive and how he smacked into a car in a store parking lot. He said the other driver had every reason to chew him out for scratching his car, but instead he talked to him like he was his son.

The kicker was that later the pastor found out the man's son had been killed in a war, and the man said the pastor reminded him a lot of his boy.

"So this last week at Safeway," the pastor continued, "I happened to be walking back to my car when a young lady pulled into the slot next to me. She cut it too close. Then I heard the creaking and scratching of metal against metal. She stopped, backed up, and the metal screeched again. When she finally parked, I found her in tears. And I remembered the man who had been so kind to me as a teenager.

"Now, I like my car. I keep it as clean and shiny as I can. When I saw the dent and scratches, it bothered me. But you know what? *Things* are temporal. Twenty years from now—maybe sooner—my car will be in a junkyard. But that young lady will probably have a family, children of her own, and she will be affected by this. So we had a long talk about insurance companies and monthly payments."

Everybody laughed. I wished Leigh could hear this, because she's not a Christian *or* a good driver.

"I could give you a hundred examples of when I haven't been patient or gracious with people," the pastor said. "But I believe what that older man did for me so many years ago allowed me to show grace to that young lady this week. You see, when *you've* been forgiven, when *you've* messed up and someone's come along and shown you grace, it's a lot easier to pass that along to your neighbor."

CHAPTER 36

❈ Ashley ❈

I thought how nice it would be if there were more people in Red Rock like this pastor. His message made sense, and I wondered if God was trying to tell me something.

After the sermon and another hymn, the pastor opened the floor for prayer requests. A few mentioned surgeries and physical problems. One woman asked for prayer for her daughter at college.

"I have something we should pray about," a man said, his voice booming from the back. I turned and recognized Hank Clashman. "I commend Pastor Shepherd for that message. It's important to show forgiveness. But it's also important to stand for something. If we don't stand for something, we'll fall for anything."

"That's right," someone said and several nodded.

"This town has fallen prey to a man who writes evil stories," Clashman continued. "He subjected children to his warped mind and then moved on to adults. I've been praying God would strike him down—and it looks like he's answered my prayers."

The church fell deathly silent. I couldn't argue with Mr. Clashman about Jake Konig's stories, but praying God would strike him down?

"The truth is," Clashman said, pointing at Mom, "this very woman in our service today has come to write the vile author's story. She's telling lies about his life so more people will read his garbage."

"Hank!" someone called out from the front, but I couldn't take my eyes off Mr. Clashman.

"She stays at the Konig castle with her kids, and yet she sits among us this morning, pretending to be a Christian while doing the devil's work."

It seemed every eye in the church was on us. Some people looked angry. Others seemed sorry. I guessed this wasn't the first time Hank Clashman had spoken out.

Mom stood. "Let's go."

"Hank!" the pastor said. "This is no way to treat a visitor. Everyone is welcome here."

"Never thought I'd be escaping from a church," Mom said as we left.

"How did he know who you were?" Bryce said.

"Who knows? He got my job wrong, anyway. Either of you two talk with anybody about what I'm doing?"

Bryce shook his head. "Just The Broken Saber guy."

Mom turned on him. "What? You told him?"

He started to explain, but she cut him off. "Tell me later. We're not going to be standing here waiting for a cab when church lets out. Start walking."

CHAPTER 37

☺ *Bryce* ☺

I was feeling terrible about having said anything to Mr. Rosel and also about not telling Mom before. When we got near The Broken Saber we showed Mom the horse stables. I asked if she wanted to see the restaurant menu and pick up a brochure.

"Yes," she said, "and then you can tell me why you felt obligated to tell a perfect stranger—"

As we crossed the road she stopped when a car pulled up to the curb. I turned, ready to fight. I wasn't about to let anybody threaten my mom.

But when the driver got out, it was a well-dressed woman in her 50s with grayish-brown hair. "Kathryn?" she said.

Mom stared, obviously puzzled. "Yes?"

"I'm Nancy Shepherd, Pastor Tim's wife. I'm so sorry about what happened. We all are. Hank Clashman is a loud-mouthed, meddling . . . I shouldn't say that. I just want you to know he doesn't speak for us."

"Well, thank you. May I ask how you know my name?"

"Let me explain over lunch. Would you and your children join us?"

CHAPTER 38

❀ Ashley ❀

The Shepherds lived in a smallish brick home about a mile from the church. They had a nice view of the mountains, and Mrs. Shepherd pointed out the national forest as we parked.

"Tim will be along," she said. She headed for the kitchen, and Mom followed to help. Bryce and I set the table. A family picture stood on the mantel over the fireplace, and it looked at least 20 years old. They had four children—three boys and a girl.

Pastor Shepherd drove up and rushed into the house. He looked relieved when he saw us. "You must be Kathryn's twins," he said, shaking our hands. "Tim Shepherd's my name."

"We know who you are," I said. "Good sermon."

"Well, thank you. I—"

I punched Bryce's shoulder. "PS and TS! Pastor Shepherd! Tim Shepherd! You're the same person."

"Excuse me?" he said.

"I'll explain," I said, "but how do you know us?"

"I'll explain," he said. "Over lunch."

We sat at the table as Mrs. Shepherd and Mom brought in the food. After asking the blessing, Pastor Shepherd said, "Jake told me about you, Kathryn, and that he was going to visit you."

"You know Jake?" Bryce said.

"We've been talking. We actually had lunch the day he disappeared. But before I get into that, I want to apologize for Hank."

"I appreciate that," Mom said, "but you don't have to answer for everyone in your church."

"He's obsessed with Jake and his writing. Every time a new Konig book or movie comes out, he protests. I know the stuff is bad, but I have a different idea of how to change things."

"Is that why you befriended Jake?" Bryce said.

"He actually came to me."

"To your church?" I said.

"No, I said things in an interview with the local paper to counteract what Hank said. Give a more balanced view. I said the church's enemy is not Jake Konig. I said I thought that, like everyone, Jake needed to know God in a personal way, but that meanwhile we shouldn't expect him to live like a Christian."

"Bet Hank loved that," Bryce said.

"He threatened to speak out against me, but we had a talk. Now what's this business about my initials?"

"We saw your initials in Jake's notes and on the Gassy Pastor video," I said.

"I hope you weren't offended."

"I think we were laughing too hard to think about it," Bryce said.

"So let me get this straight," Mom said. "You remembered my name from conversations with Jake?"

Pastor Shepherd nodded. "During our last meeting he mentioned that he had talked with you and planned to visit you. Explained who you were, that you had twins, what happened to your first husband—"

"I was so sorry to hear about that," Mrs. Shepherd said.

"Jake never made it home," Pastor Shepherd continued. "When I heard someone with twins was staying at the Konigs' house, I made the connection. I was glad to see you at our service today. Just sorry it turned out so badly."

CHAPTER 39

☺ *Bryce* ☺

"So why did Jake call you in the first place?" I said.

"He told me he appreciated what I said in the paper and that he'd like to buy me lunch."

"He was willing to be seen with you at the diner?" Ashley said.

"Not at first. We met a few miles away. As we got to know each other better, we moved to the diner and his booth."

"And he didn't care what people thought?"

"Hardly."

"Did he want to become a Christian?" Ashley said.

Pastor Shepherd stroked his chin. "I wouldn't put it that way.

I think he was intrigued at first that he was dealing with a church-man who seemed somewhat reasonable. Once he saw that I was fairly well-read and had actually seen a couple of his movies and read a few of his books, we became friends. He had a lot of spiritual questions."

"I sense that in his latest manuscript," Mom said. "What was he asking?"

"I don't feel free to talk specifics. Let's just say he was grappling with choices he's made."

"What do you think happened to him?" I said.

"I don't know, but I'll tell you this: I believe with all my heart that Jake Konig is alive."

CHAPTER 40

❀ Ashley ❀

Remembering the message on the computer screen sent shivers down my back. "I think he's alive too, Pastor," I said.

I know he didn't mean to, but he looked puzzled that I had an opinion on it. Of course, he couldn't know Bryce and I had been working on this for days.

"One of Jake's big concerns," he said, "was running out of stories. He wanted to get back the original fire in his writing. That doesn't sound like a person who wanted to end his life."

"So what happened?" Mom said. "Where is he?"

"There are people here," Pastor Shepherd said, "who have it in for him. You heard from one this morning. Then there're his family and staff. Who knows what they really think of him?" He shook his head. "Jake has a lot of enemies, and his biggest is himself."

"What do you mean?" Bryce said.

"Jake is a talented guy—brilliant mind, fantastic imagination—but he has a lot of skeletons in his closet. Some of his stories were written when he was drinking or on drugs. I think a lot of that behavior was to help him forget about what happened when he was a kid."

"Such as?" Mom said.

"He basically raised himself and his younger brother until . . ."

"Until what?" I said.

Pastor Shepherd pursed his lips. "Jake's little brother died one day while Jake was supposed to be watching him. He was playing with matches in an upstairs bedroom. It wasn't a big fire, didn't burn the house down or anything, but the smoke . . . he was found under the bed."

"How awful," Mom said. "Jake never told me that."

"That must have been why he wrote *The Fire Upstairs,*" Bryce said.

The pastor nodded. "Much of Jake's writing has been his effort to make sense of things, to deal with bad stuff that's happened."

His voice caught, and he covered his mouth. "I pray every day he'll be found alive," he managed. "That he'll walk into my office, tell me he's given his heart to God, and say he wants to write different things now."

CHAPTER 41

Bryce

Pastor Shepherd drove us back to the Konig house and stopped at the gate. We reached Gerald over the intercom (I wondered if he ever took a day off), and while we waited for him to come and let us in, the pastor told us more about his last conversation with Jake.

"Jake knew where I stood on the way he lived his life. He worried that if he stopped drinking and doing drugs his ideas would dry up. I had begun reading more and more of his work, trying to understand him better. I said, 'Jake, don't you think that's already happening *because* of the negative things in your life?'

"That seemed to get to him. It really did. He quizzed me on what I had noticed in his writing, and he pushed until I had to tell him."

"What'd you say?" I said.

The pastor cocked his head. "I was pretty frank. I told him I knew he was a best-selling writer not only because he was a horror writer but because he was a brilliant storyteller. But that frankly I thought his latest work was full of despair and rehashing old ideas. His worldview was coming through loud and clear. Characters weren't changing, weren't learning, weren't growing. I said that if he was trying to say life was empty and hopeless, he was succeeding."

"That's just what I've been thinking about his books!" I said. "I couldn't put my finger on it, but that's it. It's like all he has to say is that life is horrible and scary so get used to it."

Pastor Shepherd nodded. "I was straightforward with him. I told him that if he got to know Christ and let God work in his life, God had the power to make all things new. I said, 'Jake, you wouldn't believe the freedom and joy you'd experience. Your writing would take off like a rocket.'"

"What did he say to that?" Ashley said.

"A look came over him I've seen many times before. A person struggling under a weight and wondering if there's really a chance they can get it off their back. But Jake's lived under that weight for so long, I think it scared him to death to even think about changing. And of course he had to wonder about his reputation if he ever did something like that."

"How did you leave things with him?" Mom said.

"I didn't try to soften anything or make it easier for him. We just sat there, him wringing his hands, looking at me, looking away. Then my beeper went off, showing a call from the church office. Cell phone coverage is horrible here, so I moved to the pay phone to call.

When I got no answer I thought I'd better head back to the church to be sure everything was all right. Jake thanked me for the conversation and said he'd like to talk again the next day. I told him I'd be in all day and would love to see him."

"And that was the last you saw of him?" I said.

"The diner staff said he finished his coffee, made a few notes, paid the bill, and left."

"Anyone remember which way he headed on his cycle?" I said. "Toward home or the other way?"

"No idea."

"And was everything okay at the church?" Ashley said.

"That's the funny thing. When I got there my secretary was just getting back from lunch. She said she hadn't called, and there were no messages on our machine."

"Who else has your beeper number?" I said.

"Anybody who wants it. It's printed in our bulletin."

CHAPTER 42

❀ Ashley ❀

I called Clancy to see if we were still on for another movie at his place, but he said, "Yeah, about that. I was going to call you. I've got something else going today. Maybe another time?"

"Sure," I said, trying to hide my disappointment. I wondered if he had heard about what happened at church, or if he really did have something else going on.

I was still dying to know what kind of trouble Clancy was in at school. He had that alternative, rebel look but seemed like such a good guy at heart. . . .

I wandered outside to the front of the writing house and sat on a bench near a small pond and waterfall. I watched the big goldfish.

"Those are koi," someone said. I turned to see Gerald.

I wondered what he was doing here, but I didn't want to ask. "How big do they get?" I said.

"Huge." He pointed. "That's the oldest, Griselda. Mrs. Konig named them after characters in Jake's books." He paused. "You having a good time here?"

"Sure."

"Glad to hear it. If you need anything, please let me know. I'd be glad to run any one of you to the grocery, or if you give me a list of what you need, I'll pick it up myself."

"Thanks," I said, not sure what to think. Bryce and I hadn't known what to make of Gerald, and here he was, being as thoughtful as a person could be.

I wondered if I could get him to tell me anything about Clancy's troubles without directly asking. I said, "Sir, what school does Clancy go to in California?"

"That would be Wildmore Academy. Why do you ask?"

"Just wondering. He mentioned it."

When he was gone I went back in and sat at Jake's computer, praying no freaky messages would appear. I missed home, so I clicked on our family Web site. There was Dylan on his swing set wearing his "Future President" shirt. *If that's true, we're in big trouble,* I thought. Seeing his face made me miss him more. I had watched him wake up a few days before, something I didn't have time to do during the school year. Peeking into his room, trying to stay quiet and not laugh, I saw his arm move. Then he sang, looked out the window, and started talking to himself. Finally, I couldn't hold it any longer and I laughed out loud. He grabbed his sippy cup and blanket and the stuffed animal he'd slept with and bounded toward me, arms outstretched.

I wanted this trip to be over.

I experimented with Web addresses and finally found the Wildmore Academy home page. It showed kids playing violins and cellos, others playing polo, some studying around an oak table—all smiling. The ad said it was "an exclusive education that prepares young adults for a global community." That sounded like a boot camp for the end of the world. It boasted students from all 50 states and 75 countries.

I clicked on the admissions video. It was slick and showed kids moving into the dorms, eating in the cafeteria, playing in the orchestra, sculpting in art class. The more I watched, the more ideal it seemed. Almost not real, it looked so good. Diversity. Opportunity. Maturity. It implied that if you attended Wildmore, you'd wind up like all their alumni—successful in business, the arts, and politics.

I couldn't imagine living away from home like that, but the kids on the video smiled like they were in heaven.

I looked through all the news and press releases from the school, but the only thing I found about Clancy was an announcement that "even the prestigious novelist Jake Konig has chosen Wildmore for his own son."

I searched for a newspaper in the area, and in a blurb dated the first week of June I found what I was looking for.

Renovation of Tower Hall Planned

Wildmore, California—Three weeks after a suspicious fire in the historic Tower Hall on the Wildmore Academy campus, administration officials have released plans for renovation of the 150-year-old structure.

Wildmore Academy president, Dr. Ogden Knox, said the

repair work was scheduled to be completed before students returned in the fall.

Dr. Knox again declined to reveal details of the investigation into the blaze and rumors that a disgruntled student set the fire. "We are handling this internally and have no plans to press charges against any individual," Knox says.

CHAPTER 43

☻ *Bryce* ☻

I awoke Monday with an idea and asked Mom if I could check out Jake's computer before she started work.

"You have half an hour," she said.

I called my computer-geek friend, Kael Barnes, in Red Rock and told him we had seen a strange message on the screen a few nights before. "Could that have come from another computer someplace else?"

"Sure," Kael said. "If the computer's hooked to the Internet."

"It is."

"Then whoever did it could have been using any of a hundred different programs. Anything weird on the toolbar?"

I described the icons, and when I told him about a rotating red diamond he said, "Bingo. That's his link to the virtual network. He can access that computer from anywhere as long as he can log on to the Internet."

CHAPTER 44

❀ Ashley ❀

Bryce and I were in the golf cart heading to town when I told him what I'd found out about Clancy.

"You sure he was the one who did it?"

"Well, yeah, sure. Aren't you?"

"You're jumping to a pretty big conclusion."

"Well," I said, "I need to spend more time with him. That way maybe I'll find out more about Jake. What I found could—"

"Make him mad about you snooping around." Bryce pulled the golf cart to the side of the road. "Look, I know you like this guy."

"You mean like him as in really liking him?"

"Ash, come on. I know you. I can see it. You like him, and that's okay, but you have to remember who he is and be careful."

My stomach felt like a pretzel, and the more Bryce talked, the more twisted it became. "It's not like I'm going to marry the guy. I can't even date yet, for crying out loud!"

Bryce shook his head and punched the accelerator. "Fine!"

I folded my arms and looked away.

When he parked in town, I said I wanted to go to the bookstore. Bryce wanted to go to the diner. "Let's split up," he said.

"Fine." I stomped off.

At the bookstore I approached a lady wearing reading glasses, who was shelving books. She had golden hair and was flushed from bending over. "I've got a question about Jake Konig," I said.

She frowned. "Doesn't everyone? Isn't it a shame? He used to come and sign books here. People from all over would buy from us because they knew they could get signed copies. We'd even send them in the mail. Now the only place you can get signed Konig books is at The Broken Saber. Earl has the most extensive library, lots of first print editions. A real fan. I guess you'd have to be to buy that haunted house."

"Haunted? You're kidding, right?"

She looked over her glasses. "Honey, more people have left that place in the middle of the night than I can name. Sounds, drafts, voices. And with the history of the place, who can blame them?"

"History?"

"That's where gunslingers used to go. Many were killed there. The whole place is built over an old mine shaft. They say even the stables are haunted. I'm not sure it's true, but I wouldn't doubt it."

CHAPTER 45

😊 *Bryce* 😊

I felt bad about the rift with Ashley, but I knew *she* knew what I was saying about Clancy was true. Our youth pastor had been telling us we can and should be friends with people who aren't Christians—otherwise, who would we ever tell about our faith?—but when it comes to boy/girl stuff, it's not a good idea.

Sam and Mom love each other and do well together, but they were married before Mom became a Christian, and I can tell her heart aches for him to know God. But something's holding him back.

I sat at the counter in the diner on a round, padded stool. The place was nearly empty. I ordered a milk shake and put my pad of paper down. The waitress, a different one from before, asked if I was new in town.

I nodded. "Staying with friends. So this is where Jake Konig eats, huh?"

"Used to anyway," she said, then stopped wiping the counter and stared at me. "You're not one of those, are you?"

"One of those?"

"Gawkers. People who slow down at accident sites, looking for blood and guts."

"No, ma'am. I'm just trying to figure out what happened to him."

"Aren't we all? You should leave that to the police."

"Were you working the last time Jake was in here?"

She rolled her eyes. "No, but the cook was." She turned and hollered through a hole in the wall. "Ward? Junior Deputy out here wants to talk with you about Jake."

Ward was young, probably in his 20s. His hair was short and moussed. His long apron was as clean as if he'd just taken it out of the washing machine. He wiped his hands as he approached. "What do ya need to know, pod'ner?" Ward talked with a drawl, like he wasn't from Colorado—or was from a part of Colorado I hadn't been to yet.

"Sorry to interrupt your work, but—"

"Things are slow," he said, "but make it quick."

I asked what he remembered about Jake's last visit to the diner.

"Like I told the police, he had lunch—his usual—with the reverend, who left before Jake did. Cut outta here a few minutes later on his motorcycle, lickety-split like always."

"Which direction?"

"Back toward his house, I think. I never thought about it. Just assumed, I guess."

"So he could have gone the other way?"

"Sure, I s'pose."

"You talk to him that day?"

"Actually I did. Ran into him in the bathroom right after the reverend left. Told me he loved my food and that I could make a lot more money in one of them fancy restaurants in Denver. I said I didn't doubt it, but I wasn't going anywhere. I got a smile out of him when I said I wanted people to fall in love with diners again. He said, 'You're speaking my language, son.'"

"Anything else? He seem upset at all?"

Ward shook his head. "Don't think so. I saw him drain his coffee, pay his bill, leave a tip. He tips all right, doesn't he, Doris?"

"No complaints," she said.

"Next thing I know, people say he's missing."

"Anybody suspicious in the restaurant that day?"

He shrugged. "Not that I noticed. What do you think, Doris?"

"Me? The usual. That weird guy up at the Saber place."

"Mr. Rosel?"

"Don't know his name. I'm tired of thinking about it. Sometimes everybody in here looks suspicious to me. Like right now."

When Ward headed back to the kitchen, I asked Doris if I could sit in Jake's booth.

She sighed. "If you have to."

CHAPTER 46

❀ Ashley ❀

I found Bryce at Jake's booth in the restaurant and sat across from him. "Sorry about back there," I said. "I know you're just trying to help."

He nodded, and I told him about the woman in the bookstore. He brought me up to date and said, "The waitress thinks Mr. Rosel was in here the day Jake disappeared. Didn't he say he was at home?"

"Maybe the waitress was wrong. Or he could have come in later."

Bryce tapped the table with a finger. "What if the message that came over the computer wasn't preprogrammed? What if Jake is trying to talk to us?"

"From the dead?" I said.

"Come on, I'm serious. Kael says someone could access Jake's computer from the Internet. He could be trying to send us a message from anywhere."

That thought hit home. "Or next door," I said.

Bryce's eyes widened. "Yeah, what if somebody like . . . Gerald did something to him?"

"Where does he live?"

Bryce shrugged.

"Say Gerald has him locked away somewhere and walked in on him while he was trying to send the message?" I said.

"Yeah, but what's Gerald's motive for kidnapping his own boss?"

"I don't know," I said. "Maybe he's got a thing for Mrs. Konig. Or maybe Gerald wants revenge—Clancy said Gerald and his dad argued a lot."

Bryce ran a hand through his hair. "I've been trying to eliminate people, but this whole town is filled with suspects."

CHAPTER 47

☺ *Bryce* ☺

We called Clancy, who told us Gerald lived in a house the Konigs had bought when they first purchased the hillside property, before they moved into the mansion. "They bought several houses nearby and demolished them so there wouldn't be anyone living too close," he said. Which made me wonder if someone who had lived in one of those houses was mad at Jake for tearing them down.

Clancy told us where Gerald's place was. "He's running an errand for my mom right now. You guys gonna watch another movie over here?"

"Yeah, where were you yesterday?"

"Had to go somewhere with my mom. Call me and we'll watch something tonight."

Gerald's house was a small two-story with gabled windows. We rode the golf cart up his gravel driveway and parked near the porch. A detached garage in the back looked a hundred years old, its roof leaning and shingles falling.

"What if he finds us here?" Ashley said. "We going to tell him we were just checking to see if he'd hidden Jake inside?"

"I'll think of something," I said. "Go look in the garage."

"The police had to have already combed this place, right?"

"Probably. But let's see for ourselves."

I stepped onto the porch as Ashley left. The boards creaked, and a rocking chair by the front door was so rickety it looked like it wouldn't even hold Dylan. I rubbed dust off the front window to get a look inside. There was a small TV on a box in the corner and a stereo with CDs lying around. A big La-Z-Boy chair was it as far as furniture. A stairway ran up the left side of the room.

I opened the screen door and knocked just in case. To my surprise, the door was unlocked. I was going in, and I could hear my own heart.

Something moved in the corner of my eye, and Ashley jumped up onto the porch.

"Don't *do* that!" I whispered.

"Do what? There's nothing in the garage except an old car covered by some sort of tarp. Bryce, what are you doing? What if he comes back?"

"What if Jake is in here?" I said.

"You can't justify breaking into somebody's house just because—"

"It's unlocked! I'm not breaking anything."

"But still—"

"Ash, you're such a girl."

"You know I'm right, and don't tell me they can't do anything to us because we're only 13. Gerald could sue Mom for raising delinquent children or something. Plus, they'd never let us ride the golf cart again."

That was the best reason yet, but she wasn't finished. She saved the biggest weapon for last.

"Besides, you think Jesus would walk into someone's house like this?"

I nearly doubled over, cackling.

"What's so funny?" Ashley said.

"Thinking about Jesus as a private detective with one of those trench coats and a wide-brimmed hat."

"You're evil," she said.

I shook my head and closed the door. Ashley was right. We couldn't walk into someone's house unless someone was dying in there.

We were headed back to the golf cart when Ashley lightly touched my arm and spoke softly. "Don't look back, but we're being watched."

When I hopped in the cart I noticed a car parked by the road. Someone inside was watching us with binoculars.

CHAPTER 48

✖ Ashley ✖

Mom seemed distracted at dinner that evening. She moved her macaroni and cheese around like she was building a new roadway on her plate.

"Is it Jake's story?" I said to Mom.

"What?" She looked up from the Kraft Freeway.

"Something's on your mind."

"Oh, that's part of it. Another part of me wonders if I did the right thing taking this job. It's going to help moneywise, but I wonder what it's really going to cost."

"Didn't the pastor back home say it was a good idea?" Bryce said.

"Not exactly. He said it was a decision he couldn't make for me."

We ate in silence until Bryce said, "You're not thinking about going home, are you?"

"I'm going to give it a few more days, but you and Ashley can go back if you want."

"No!" Bryce said.

"We want to stay and see it through," I said.

"Plus," he said, "you promised we could stay at The Broken Saber before we leave."

Mom nodded. "I guess I did. Why don't you call and see if you can arrange it."

Bryce beat me to the phone and left a message on Mr. Rosel's machine. Then I called Clancy and told him Bryce and I would be over with a movie at seven.

For some reason Clancy didn't seem too excited about it, but I wanted to get more information. Plus, Bryce had an idea.

CHAPTER 49

☺ *Bryce* ☺

We picked up a DVD of an old Marx Brothers movie that is probably the funniest thing I've ever seen. My real dad introduced me to
it. Groucho's jokes are hilarious, Harpo chases people around a ship
and pretends to sing with an old record player, and Chico talks with
a funny accent and pretends to be a barber.

"An old black-and-white comedy?" Clancy said. "Please."

"Give it 20 minutes," I said. "Then if you don't like it, fine."

He shrugged and put it in the machine, but before it started, I ex-
cused myself to go to the bathroom.

Mrs. Konig was away, and Clancy had sent Caroline home.

I hurried through all the downstairs rooms I could find, listening and looking for clues. I couldn't imagine Clancy inviting us over if he had his dad stashed here somewhere, but I found a door that led to another level Clancy had never told us about. I flicked the light on and climbed the stairs carefully. I found what looked like an office identical to the one Jake had in his writing house. Same chair, same desk, same filing cabinets.

The screen saver on the monitor was running weird designs. I touched the mouse and a page came up. It looked like the outline of a new novel.

"Excuse me?"

I whirled to see Clancy in the doorway with Ashley behind him giving me one of those I-would-have-told-you-if-I-could looks.

"I . . . uh, was looking for the bathroom and found this."

"Right," Clancy said, striding past me and flicking off the monitor.

"This looks just like Jake's office," Ashley said.

"I'd like you two to leave."

"Clancy, please," I said. "I didn't mean to snoop—"

"That's exactly what you and your sister are. Snoops. Now take your stupid movie and get out."

CHAPTER 50

✖ Ashley ✖

When somebody orders you out of his house and does it with a scowl that would frighten animals, you don't ask questions. Bryce grabbed the DVD from the player, and Clancy followed us upstairs.

"What were you looking for anyway, Timberline?"

"Your dad, of course."

"You think he's here?"

"He's somewhere with computer access—or at least he was. We think he tried to contact us."

Clancy suddenly looked terrified.

"You already know this," I said. "We told you words flashed on the screen asking for help."

Clancy slumped against the wall and stumbled toward the kitchen. He dropped into a chair.

"What's the matter?" Bryce said.

Clancy stared straight ahead with hollow eyes. "I never thought it was Dad, but he said he would do that. Said he would get in touch any way he could."

"That means he's alive," I said.

Clancy shook his head. "It means he's dead. He said he would look for a way to communicate when he was gone. Guess he found it."

Neither Bryce nor I believe in ghosts or the dead communicating from the great beyond, but I could tell we weren't going to convince Clancy. And a theology lesson right then was probably not what Jesus would do.

Bryce knelt. "Look, I thought you said you'd be better off if your dad was gone."

"I was just being a smart aleck because I believed he was hiding. I never thought, till now, that he might actually have died."

"If you know anything that might help, tell us."

Clancy stared at the wall. "You found Dad's old office. When he and Mom started having problems, he built the writing house and moved there. After he disappeared, I started writing stories of my own. I figured if he could use my life in his books, why couldn't I write something?"

"Did you inherit his talent?" I said.

"Nah. It's trash. Guess I should drink and take drugs. Maybe that would help."

"You know better than that," Bryce said.

Clancy left us and we walked outside. When I first saw the main house, I had wished I lived there. Now it just looked lonely.

CHAPTER 51

☺ *Bryce* ☺

When Mr. Rosel never called back, Ashley and I decided to visit him at The Broken Saber the next day. Gerald was nowhere in sight as we zoomed down the hill in the golf cart, Ashley driving.

Halfway into town I said, "Doesn't that look like the car we saw yesterday?"

"It is," she said.

She slowed, and before she stopped I was out and crossing the road. Whoever was inside wasn't expecting this. The man had a long-billed baseball cap pulled low over his eyes. His window was open and he looked up, startled, and tried to start the old car. The engine cranked and sputtered as I reached him and slammed my hands on the roof.

"Hank Clashman!" Ashley said.

The car roared to life, but not before I noticed a pair of binoculars on the seat beside him along with some worn copies of Jake Konig's books. Alongside them were a few other familiar titles I'd seen in my mom's study back home. *Her* books.

Mom writes some books under the name Virginia Caldwell. They aren't the huge best sellers Jake writes, but they do pretty well in Christian bookstores. She hadn't published a new book in a while, and I figured that was one of the reasons things were tight at home.

"What do you kids think you're doing," Clashman said, "trying to scare me!"

"Why are you spying on us?" Ashley said, and there wasn't a hint of a quiver in her voice.

"Spying on you? Where do you get that?"

"You were watching us yesterday," I said.

"Feeling guilty for breaking into that man's house?" he said, sneering.

"We're just trying to find Mr. Konig," Ashley said.

"'Let the dead bury their dead,'" Mr. Clashman said. "And tell your mother to pack up and head home. She's going to come to no good up here."

Ashley said, "What are you doing with all those Konig books? You read them, don't you? You read them like everyone else."

"They're research. You have to know what the enemy's up to." He squinted. "Something else you can tell your mother: if her readers find out she's here, you think they'll forgive her? They'll never read her books again!"

Clashman put his car in gear, gritted his teeth, and pointed at us. "Your mother needs to stop right now or every church in the country and every Christian bookstore will know *exactly* what she's up to."

CHAPTER 52

❀ Ashley ❀

Mom swiveled back from the computer as we spilled the story. She took a deep breath. "Well, I got myself into this."

She phoned Pastor Shepherd, but his secretary told Mom he was out and that she would have him call.

Bryce and I were on our way out the door to The Broken Saber when Mom screamed.

We raced back up the stairs and burst into the office. Mom sat staring at the computer with both hands over her mouth.

The screen was rimmed with a red border and bore this message:

> *Your children are in danger.*
> *Leave now before someone gets hurt.*

Bryce reddened and ran downstairs, calling over his shoulder, "This is Clancy's work. It has to be about last night."

I followed him to the golf cart, and we zoomed down the path. He slammed on the brakes.

"The Timberlines just left their mark," I said.

Bryce jumped out, sprinted to the back of the house, and knocked. Caroline opened the door with a grim look. She must have heard the brakes.

Before she could say anything, Bryce said, "I need to talk with Clancy."

"Well, you'll need someone to drive you to the airport then. He and his mother are gone."

"Where?"

Caroline's eyes narrowed. "That's none of your business."

CHAPTER 53

◔ *Bryce* ◔

When we got back to the writing house, Mom said the pastor had called and suggested we meet in an hour at the diner. She went back to the computer, but Ashley and I soon heard her gasp.

"What?" Ashley said. "Not again! Another message?"

"No," Mom said. "The book—it's gone. It was in the main document folder and now it's not."

I helped her pull up other possible locations, but we found nothing.

"Maybe Jake erased it remotely," I said. "That's your only copy?"

Mom stared at me. "How would he know I'm working on it, and even if he did, why would he delete it?"

"What if it's Jake," I said, "but he's gone loony?"

"And he's watching us?" Ashley said. "That's eerie."

"Maybe he was really close to becoming a Christian, and something snapped."

"Let's see what Pastor Shepherd thinks."

He was waiting for us in the Jake Konig booth.

When we told him what Hank Clashman had said, Pastor Shepherd shook his head. Then Mom told him about the erased manuscript.

"How many people know what you're doing?" he said.

"Only Mr. Rosel at The Broken Saber," she said. "Maybe I should have holed up inside there. But Bryce has another theory."

Pastor Shepherd disagreed with my idea that Jake might have gone haywire. "I can't imagine him going over the edge like that," he said. "If you'd have seen him here with me, talked with him, I don't think you'd conclude that he's gone . . . well, mad. Now I'm curious as to how much you told Mr. Rosel."

"We told him Mom was a writer but not what she was doing."

Pastor Shepherd sat back. "I'll meet with Hank Clashman tonight. And, Kathryn, if you'd feel safer, the three of you are welcome to stay with my wife and me."

"Oh, no thanks. We're fine."

"Wait," Ashley said. "If there's no manuscript, we can go home."

Mom looked down and grinned, and I knew something was up. She hadn't acted as horrified about the missing computer files as I expected, and I was about to find out why.

Mom glanced around and quietly opened her purse. "I made a backup copy. I always do, since learning the hard way that I should." She produced a small disk.

We stared at it like it was a million-dollar bill.

"Why don't you print that and bring it to my office for safekeeping," the pastor said.

CHAPTER 54

Ashley

As we drove back along the path, Mom kept looking behind us, watching for anyone suspicious. Bryce pulled into The Broken Saber parking lot.

"Looks like a place a horror writer would get inspiration," Mom said.

We knocked on the front door, but no one came. We were about to check the stables when Mr. Rosel approached, carrying a couple of cans of paint. "Thought I heard someone drive up."

He put the paint down, wiped his hands on his shirt, and shook

Mom's hand. "Earl Rosel. I met your children the other day, Kathryn. They tell me you're a writer."

Mom smiled. "And they tell me you're a big fan of Jake."

"I have at least 10 copies of everything he's written. Many autographed by the author himself."

"We were wondering if you might let us stay a night. We may not be here much longer."

"Really?" There was something strange in his voice, almost like he was pleased. "In that case, how about tonight?" He looked at us like he was giving us a gold coin.

Mom laughed. "Wonderful. How much would it cost?"

"Oh, posh," he said, waving. "It would be my honor. My cook is off until the renovation is complete, but I'll whip something up for dinner and breakfast tomorrow."

"Great," Mom said. "What time would you like us?"

He looked at his watch. "How about dinner at six, and then I'll give you the ghost tour before bedtime?"

"Ghost tour?" I said.

He smiled. "I promise to take it easy on the faint of heart."

CHAPTER 55

☺ *Bryce* ☺

I helped print the manuscript, which took almost two whole reams of paper. I pulled the disk out as the printer *whirr*ed, making sure nothing happened to the file. I grabbed a black trash bag from under the sink and wrapped the pages in it. Then I hopped in the golf cart and delivered it to the church.

I knew Mom still had the backup disk, but I pretended what I was carrying was the only copy and worth a lot of money. Now I know how those Brinks truck drivers feel. I kept looking back to see if anyone was following.

I imagined I saw a car in the church parking lot, but when I got there it was empty except for the secretary's car. Pastor Shepherd wasn't there, but his secretary said she was expecting me and put the bag on the pastor's desk.

CHAPTER 56

✖ Ashley ✖

When we pulled up to The Broken Saber just before six, candles were burning in the front window.

Bryce carried our suitcases inside, where Mr. Rosel had set four places at the dining-room table. The plates and silverware looked expensive, and the glasses sparkled in the candlelight. Mr. Rosel poured Bryce and me sparkling grape juice and himself wine, offering Mom the same. She said grape juice was fine for her too.

He brought out a huge salad and stuffed mushrooms. I was full by the time I was done with the salad. Then he served tiny potatoes, fresh garlic green beans, and steak that made my mouth water.

"You don't need a cook," Bryce said. "This is great!"

Mr. Rosel laughed. "We do get comments on our cuisine, but most people come here because of the Konig connection."

"Speaking of that," Bryce said, "do you remember where you were the day he disappeared?"

"Certainly. I was right here at the inn. All day, in fact. Except for a few minutes when I had to run to the diner for a pie."

After dessert Mr. Rosel offered Mom coffee and took us into a sitting room that had a fireplace, couches and chairs, a television, and an old piano. A bookshelf in the corner had copies of crackly old books, along with a few recent Jake Konig titles.

"Why don't you play something, Ashley?" Mom said, lifting the cover off the piano keys.

"Yes, yes, go ahead," Mr. Rosel said.

Bryce rolled his eyes, but I didn't mind. I had memorized several songs from my recitals over the years and chose "Solfeggietto" by Carl Philipp Emanuel Bach. I guess when you can write music like that you need four names. They all clapped when I finished.

Then Mr. Rosel brought out pecan pie à la mode. After that I wasn't sure I could move, let alone go on the ghost tour.

CHAPTER 57

☻ *Bryce* ☻

I couldn't wait for the tour, even though my stomach felt like it had a pecan football in it. I carried our suitcases upstairs, and Mr. Rosel unlocked the door to a spacious room with two beds, a small desk in front of a window that overlooked the courtyard and the stables, a fireplace, and a walk-in closet.

"Ashley, you and your mother will be in here," he said. "Bryce, you'll be in the adjoining suite."

A door near the closet led to my room. It was smaller but had its own TV and a big bed with poufy covers. The ceiling looked 50 feet high, and old photos and drawings hung on the wall.

"The tour starts here," Mr. Rosel said, motioning to a black-and-white photo of a pretty woman in a pioneer dress. "This was the first owner, Clara Biggswell. Her father fought in the Civil War, and his saber hung over the front door. Clara tried her hand at gold prospecting but found there was more money in feeding and boarding miners. She rented rooms out at 25 cents a night. She was a shrewd businesswoman. Tough as nails. She loved riding her white horse through the hills."

"What became of her?" Ashley said.

He pointed out the window. "See that water well? They found her at the bottom, her money stolen, the saber above the door broken in half. The thieves even took her horse. Legend says the horse threw one thief as they rode around the mountain. The others got away."

"Scary," Ashley said.

"Not half as scary as the sight many still see on moonlit nights . . . a hooded figure riding a white horse through the woods."

I quietly stepped behind Ashley and said, "Boo!"

She jumped and let out a yelp.

I moved quickly to the desk, keeping my distance. "What about Jake?" I said. "Isn't this the room—?"

"Yes, where he came up with the idea for *Corridor of Blood*. If you've read the book, you know it's different from the movie. Jake swore he saw something staring at him through that very window."

Mom shuddered and rubbed her arms.

"Don't worry," I said. "Anyone comes by tonight and we'll offer them pecan pie."

No one laughed.

Mr. Rosel continued, though I could tell Mom and Ashley didn't want him to. "Clara's house was bought and sold several times, fell into disrepair, and finally burned to the ground in 1913. A few years later a veteran of World War I bought the property and started building this house. It took seven years and went through many different builders. That's why you see strange angles and corners here and there."

He ran his hand along a wooden railing. "Lots of stories waiting to be told about this old house."

CHAPTER 58

Ashley

By the time Mr. Rosel finished showing us the second floor, I had had enough. Every time I passed a window I thought I saw someone on a white horse in the woods.

He told about a gunslinger shot in a chair that still had a nick from the bullet. Another story concerned a caretaker who had poisoned travelers with a special gravy recipe. "They never complained once about the meal," Mr. Rosel said.

But the story that really got me was about twin boys who haunted the third floor. Mr. Rosel told us not to go up there. "They sometimes get angry with visitors."

"What happened to them?" Bryce said. "Were they big gravy eaters?"

Bigmouth, I thought. *You had to ask, didn't you?*

Mr. Rosel told us they died in one of the laundry chutes that lead to the basement. I wanted to plug my ears and hum "The Star-Spangled Banner" or something.

"Can we see your collection of Jake's books?" I said, trying to distract him.

"Sure. That's the only room that hasn't been affected by ghosts. Maybe they're scared to go in." He chuckled as we followed him downstairs.

It was cooler down there. "I had this room added especially for my collection," Mr. Rosel said. He punched in a code on the door. I saw the first three numbers, 4-1-7, but he moved and I didn't see the last two.

When he opened the door, the air *whoosh*ed and he explained that the room was sealed and had a special heating and cooling system that kept humidity out.

The room was about 20 feet long and 10 feet wide with bookshelves built into the walls. Every shelf was filled with Jake Konig books and memorabilia. Mr. Rosel had framed pictures of Jake, magazines with Jake's picture on the covers, and even movie posters of films based on Jake's books.

Bryce reached for a book, and Mr. Rosel flinched. "I'll have to ask you to refrain from touching them."

The most expensive items, including the oldest original manuscripts, lay in a glass case.

"How much are these worth?" Bryce said.

"I had them appraised last year at almost a million dollars. It's probably more now."

"I've never seen a million dollars' worth of books," Mom said.

Mr. Rosel turned. "If I might ask, ma'am, why are you visiting the Konig estate?"

Mom said something about being old friends with Jake and doing some editorial work. I guess it satisfied him. He put on a pair of white gloves. "Here is my prized possession."

He pulled out a case and opened the top. Inside was a velvet-lined box with gilded edges. In the middle was a lined yellow pad. The pages were filled with scrawling handwriting in green ink.

"It's the first draft of the first chapter of *Corridor of Blood*," Mr. Rosel said breathlessly.

"How'd you get it?" Bryce said.

"An auction. It's the most expensive item in the room."

Mom scanned the page. "Amazing that he wrote it in longhand."

"He composed the whole thing at the desk in your room," Mr. Rosel said. "Perhaps you'll get inspiration there as well."

CHAPTER 59

☺ *Bryce* ☺

Mom locked the door as soon as we got inside our suite.

Ashley jumped onto the bed and threw the covers over her head. "I don't think it was a very good idea coming here," she said, her voice muffled.

"Just wait till those twins ask you to play checkers," I said.

"Stop it!"

"Bet they're good at flashlight tag."

"Bryce, don't," Ashley said. "I don't want to think about those twins!"

In my room I flipped on the TV. The Cubs were on their West Coast tour, tonight in San Diego. At about the sixth inning I realized I hadn't heard anything from the other room in a while, so I tiptoed to the door and peeked in. Mom and Ashley were asleep.

I tried to concentrate on the game, but my eyelids drooped. I got under the covers and propped myself up with the pillows.

Then I heard it.

It started faint and low, like air through a paper-towel tube. I figured it was outside, the wind maybe. Then it got louder. And sounded more human. A low moan.

I slipped out from under the covers and stood barefoot on the hardwood floor. Should I look under the bed? No, I couldn't think that way.

The sound seemed to be coming from the corner. By the window was a heating vent. I didn't want to look out, imagining the woman on the horse or the twins playing. I ignored the window and leaned over the vent, listening.

Cold air washed over my face. And I heard someone cry, "Help me. . . ."

CHAPTER 60

❀ Ashley ❀

"Bryce, you're scaring me," I said, coming out of the fog. I had been dreaming that I was in an old castle waiting for a knight to save me. I looked from a stone window through a mist on the moor, waiting for a horse's hoofbeats.

"Seriously, I heard someone," Bryce whispered. "Through the vent."

Bryce tries to act cool and make light of stuff that scares him. When our dad died, Bryce tried hard not to show emotion. But I remember standing outside his door at night, hearing him cry. And now I could tell he wasn't joking.

It was nearly midnight when I crept out of bed and we tiptoed into Bryce's room. He pointed at the heating vent, then put a finger to his lips. We were so still we could have heard mice snoring. I stood there a full two minutes, straining to hear anything, but there was nothing but the creaks and groans of an old house.

I yawned and shrugged.

Bryce grabbed my arm. "Ash, I swear I heard something."

"I believe you, but it's—"

Something banged—something metal. There was a faint scratching, then a low voice whimpering. I looked at Bryce with wide eyes. I wanted to get out of here and not stop until we were back in Red Rock.

"No!" a man's voice shouted. "Please, no!"

CHAPTER 61

☻ *Bryce* ☻

Ashley and I made our way out of the room without waking Mom, then down the creaky staircase. We huddled like scared cats. There was a light on in the sitting room, but no one was there.

"Where does Rosel sleep?" Ashley said.

"He's got about a hundred rooms to choose from."

"Mr. Rosel?" Ashley called in a clear voice that cut through the night.

We waited.

Nothing.

I moved to the front door, unlocked and opened it, and leaned on the doorbell. A gong overhead reminded me of a bell in one of those huge churches in Europe.

I heard footsteps. A door closed. Then I spotted Mr. Rosel on the stairs in a long, plush robe that almost reached the floor. "What's the problem?"

"We heard someone," I said.

Mr. Rosel pressed his lips together and squinted. It might have been a smile, but it looked more like he was amused with us. "My room is right above yours," he said. "I was watching a movie and probably had the volume too high."

Ashley glanced at me and frowned. It wasn't a movie, and we both knew it. It was a real person.

"I'll keep the sound down. Sorry for the inconvenience."

CHAPTER 62

✖ Ashley ✖

Mr. Rosel made me think twice, but I could tell Bryce wasn't buying his story. We climbed back to Bryce's room, but there was no way I was going to close my eyes in this place. We sat on Bryce's bed and tried to watch *SportsCenter* with the sound down. I couldn't concentrate.

"Why do you think Clancy and his mom left?" Bryce said.

I shrugged. "Maybe they had enough of us. You know how Clancy felt."

"You still like him?"

I stared Bryce down. "I care about Clancy as a human being. It doesn't go beyond that."

We sat silent and yawning for 20 minutes, and I was changing my mind about going back to bed when Bryce whispered, "Did you hear that? Like something pecking."

Tap, tap, tap.

CHAPTER 63

☻ *Bryce* ☻

I didn't have the stomach to just peek. I knew it couldn't be a person because we were too far from the ground. Could it have been a bat or a moth?

I flung open the curtains and fell back at the sight of two glowing red eyes. Ashley froze. I made myself look again. The eyes appeared human. They faded and disappeared into the darkness.

Ashley sat back on the bed, trembling. "What was that?"

I shook my head. "I don't know, but this place is getting scarier every minute."

Someone knocked, and Ashley jumped off the bed. I opened the door slowly and found Mr. Rosel in his robe and slippers, wringing his hands.

"I couldn't help hearing some commotion. It wasn't a mouse, was it? I thought I'd taken care of them all—"

"No, sir. It was something outside."

"We saw two red eyes in the window," Ashley said.

"Eyes?" Mr. Rosel said. "Oh, dear."

"What?" I said.

"It's nothing. Just another of the stories—the legends about the house."

"Tell us."

"If I may," he said, stepping inside and opening a desk drawer. He pulled out a black-and-white photo of a man holding a gun near the stables. It looked like they had recently been built.

"Archie McMillan was a regular at The Broken Saber in the late 1800s, a gold prospector with a lot of money. He was on his way here when a snowstorm hit. His horse hurt its leg, and Archie had to leave it. The snowstorm was blinding, and he may have thought he had reached the inn. People in the area said they heard tapping, as if someone were trying to get in. The next day they found him frozen. His eyes were open. And they were red."

"You think that's what we saw?" I said.

"I'm simply telling you the story. If there's anything I can do . . ."

"There is," Mom said, startling us all by appearing in the doorway. "You could drive us back to the Konig estate. Right now."

CHAPTER 64

❀ Ashley ❀

I never thought I'd be glad to be back at the writing house, but anywhere was better than The Broken Saber. Caroline buzzed us through the gate. It was a long walk up that path, and I kept thinking I heard someone in the woods.

I don't mind being scared at the movies. And it's thrilling to step onto an amusement-park ride and scream your way to the end. But this kind of fear—the real thing—wasn't good. If I never saw another pair of red eyes, it would be too soon.

The three of us sat in the living room. "What do you think we saw, Mom?"

She shook her head. "I know enough about the supernatural that I don't want to mess with it. It could have been some kind of an animal or a reflection in the window, but if both of you say it looked human . . ."

"I wonder if this is why Clancy and his mom left," Bryce said. "Maybe they saw something too."

"Let's get out of here, Mom," I said. "Let's call Sam and have him fly us home."

"There's no airport within—"

"Then have him drive. The only thing keeping us here is the book, and you can work on it at home."

Mom bit her lip. "You're right. But Bryce, you'd better make me another copy of the disk, just in case. Other than the printed one, this is all we have."

Mom unzipped her purse and fumbled through it, pulling out her checkbook and wallet. Then she dumped the contents into her lap. Gum. Eyeliner. Cell phone. A pad of paper.

But no disk.

CHAPTER 65

☺ *Bryce* ☺

The missing disk changed everything. We retraced our steps, trying to remember everywhere we'd been and everybody we'd seen the day before:

Pastor Shepherd
Ward, the cook at the diner
Earl Rosel
Caroline
Hank Clashman
Someone else?

"I left my purse in our room at The Broken Saber during dinner and the tour, but we were with Mr. Rosel the whole time."

"He could be working with someone," Ashley said. "He couldn't have done all that cooking and serving and preparing our rooms himself, could he?"

"Did he have time to race upstairs and rifle your purse while we thought he was in the kitchen bringing out another course?"

We couldn't imagine. But we had to find out who had that disk.

I tossed and turned in bed, the red eyes haunting me. Something about them didn't make sense unless you believed in ghosts, and I didn't. At least I didn't think I did.

I woke to buzzing and had to remind myself where I was. I hurried to the living room, where Mom was on the phone. Sunlight beamed from the far hill, and the clouds were tinged orange and red. I remembered something my real dad had said when we lived in Illinois: "Red sky at morning, sailors take warning." Once a tornado ripped through a town close to us after a red morning. I wondered if that saying was true in the mountains.

"We're fine. What is it?" Mom said into the phone.

Ashley plopped on the couch, puffy eyed. She looked like she'd gotten about as much sleep as I had.

"You're kidding," Mom said.

"Who is it?" I mouthed.

Mom waved. "How long ago did you find out? How could that have happened? It doesn't make sense."

Ashley sat unmoving, as if she could have dropped back off to sleep any second.

"You and Mom just get up?" I said.

She nodded. "The phone woke us."

"Well, we need to call the police then, sir," Mom said. "Last night the disk was stolen and—" She walked to the front window, rubbing her neck with her free hand. "I understand your concern, but we're talking about millions of dollars' worth—All right, I'll wait until I hear from you."

She clicked the phone off and stared out the window. "That was Pastor Shepherd. Someone broke into his office last night."

"Don't say it," Ashley said.

Mom nodded. "They stole the manuscript."

"And he doesn't want us to call the police?" I said.

"He thinks he knows who did it and is afraid it would hurt the church if we get the police involved."

CHAPTER 66

❀ Ashley ❀

Waiting was a bad idea, church reputation or not. The thief would just have that much longer to get away or hide the evidence.

"Mom, am I wrong to wonder whether Pastor Shepherd himself might be—?"

"The thief?" she said. "It crossed my mind. He was the only one who knew all the information. We didn't tell anybody else about the disk, and keeping the manuscript safe for me was his idea."

Bryce scratched his head. "Then why would he tell us it was stolen? Why not let us think it's still safe with him until we ask for it? Or make a copy of it so when you take the original, he still has one?"

"I don't see how he could be in on this," I said. "He seemed so genuine about Jake."

"How do we know he's telling the truth?" Bryce said. "Clancy thought it was impossible his dad was interested in spiritual stuff."

"That doesn't mean it couldn't happen," I said. "If Jake was thinking about God, he wouldn't announce it."

Someone knocked at the front door.

CHAPTER 67

Bryce

"Sorry to bother you this early," Clancy said. "I heard you come in last night and wondered . . . well, Mom wondered if there was anything wrong."

"Thought you were out of town," I said.

"Mom and I got back late yesterday afternoon."

I told him we had hoped to stay at The Broken Saber the night before. "But it didn't work out. Let's just say we didn't feel all that comfortable."

Clancy said, "Mom was also wondering about your work, ma'am. How's it coming?"

Mom hesitated. "I'm making progress. I hope everyone likes what I've done."

"I'll tell her. Listen, would you mind if I took a walk with Ashley for a few minutes?"

CHAPTER 68

❋ Ashley ❋

Clancy and I walked past the tennis court and around the mountain on a path that looked like it was made by deer. I saw large hoofprints and pellets that looked like rabbit droppings.

Clancy led me past a grove of pines and up to the top of a rock outcropping. The last 300 yards were the toughest because they went straight up the mountain, but Clancy looked like he had done this a million times.

The whole thing reminded me of the rocks our town was named after, though these boulders were more gray and brown than red. The view took my breath away. The waterfall was so white it looked like milk chugging out of the rocks. The town was quaint and pictur-esque, and I could even see the gloomy Broken Saber.

The higher we climbed the harder it was to breathe, and I was glad I didn't have to huff and puff through small talk.

"This is where I come to think," Clancy said, pointing to a huge rock that looked like an easy chair. We sat and faced the falls. I could barely hear the water splashing in the distance.

I couldn't fight back a twinge of fear. What if Clancy had done something to his dad? What if he had hurt his mom on their trip the day before and brought me here to push me off? It didn't make sense, but . . .

"I wanted to apologize for being a dork the other day," he said. "I know you and Bryce care about my dad. I shouldn't have jumped on you like I did."

"Thanks."

"And I wanted to tell you the truth about where I was yesterday."

"You don't have to—"

"No, I want to. My mom and I went to my school . . . to clear things up. Not sure they believed me, though. In fact, I'm pretty sure they didn't."

"Believe you?"

"One of my friends is the son of . . . well, a famous politician. We were fooling around up in an old tower one night, just having fun, when he suggested we start a fire. I told him he was crazy, but he said they needed to replace the thing anyway and that this way the insurance company would pay for it instead of the alumni. He said people would thank us, though we couldn't ever tell anybody."

"So how could they thank you? That makes no sense."

"Tell me about it."

"Did you start it?" I said.

"No. I told him my dad could pay for it without batting an eye. Seemed stupid to me."

"So you watched? That makes you just as—"

"No! I left. I even told him I was going to call security and tell them what he was doing if he didn't come with me. Of course, I was bluffing, but I should have called them. A few minutes later I saw smoke and flames from the tower. I called the fire department but didn't identify myself."

"So what happened when you went back?"

"Someone saw me running from the tower, and the fire department traced the alarm call to my dorm. I got accused, but naturally they couldn't get me to admit it and they had no real evidence."

"Why didn't you tell them the truth?"

"I couldn't rat out my friend. But my mom told me that if I want to return in the fall, I needed to tell them the whole story. I love the school and my friends, and I really wanted to go back, but I refused."

"You went there yesterday and yet still didn't—"

"The reason we went was because they said they finally had evidence that proved I did it. My friend, the one who did it, had talked to them. He said I had started the fire."

"And they believed him?"

"I spilled the story. Some wanted to believe me, I think, but I guess it's better for them to blame it on some horror novelist's son than the son of a guy who might become president."

"Politics," I said. "You're not going back?"

Clancy shook his head. "I can't see how."

"That's awful," I said. "I know a guy who was accused of something, and he was innocent."

"Bet he was ticked."

"He's a good friend of mine. I hope you get to meet him."

CHAPTER 69

☻ *Bryce* ☻

I kept looking at my left wrist, but I'd misplaced my watch. I figured I had left it at The Broken Saber. I usually take it off and strap it to the headboard of my bed at night. In the confusion of the noises and red eyes, I'd left it. At least that's what I thought.

When Ashley returned, I asked her to help me find my watch. We rode the golf cart down the path, and she pointed out the rocks she and Clancy had climbed. And she told me his story.

The Broken Saber looked like a sad sack of lumber to me. We walked around to below where my window was the night before. No way anyone could have gotten that high and peered in. The ground was soft and mushy because of a small pond, so no one could have stood on a ladder.

A chimney ran up that side of the house, and on top was some kind of antenna. That was strange, since there was a satellite dish back near the stables.

I noticed something on the eave, just above the next floor. Someone had affixed a small pulley outside the window—the window above my room.

"You going in?" Ashley said. "See if Mr. Rosel found your watch?"

"Yeah, but I'd sure like to get a closer look at that thing on the eave. You still remember the combination to the book room downstairs?"

"The first three numbers were 4-1-7, but I didn't see the last two. But that's a long way from the third floor."

I put a finger in the air. "I think I have it."

"You're not going down there," Ashley said. "I don't think Mr. Rosel would like you snooping around a million dollars' worth of books. Plus, you might see the red eyes again."

I put a hand on her shoulder. "I'll hide while you ring the bell. Go for my watch and I'll meet you—"

The front door swung open, and Mr. Rosel stepped out. "May I help you?"

CHAPTER 70

✖ Ashley ✖

I was glad Mr. Rosel had surprised us and that Bryce wasn't going to snoop around and make me go to that terrifying room alone.

"I left my watch in the room," Bryce said.

Mr. Rosel smiled, but it looked more like a wince. "I'm sorry, but I have the exterminators coming in a few minutes."

"I know right where it is. I take it off every night, and—"

"All right," Mr. Rosel said, waving, "but hurry."

He handed Bryce a key and stared at us as we jogged up the winding stairs. Bryce's hands shook when he put the key in the door. The beds were still unmade. I found his watch right where he said it would be and loosened the band. Bryce had gone straight to the window, raised it, and leaned out, examining something. "Right there," he said. "Looks like some kind of pulley."

"Great," I said, handing him the watch. "Now can we go?"

"Look, Ash, there's something hanging on the pulley."

"C'mon, Mr. Rosel's waiting." But I did see a clear plastic string. "Looks like fishing wire."

"Find what you were looking for?" Mr. Rosel said from behind us.

I yipped and turned to face him.

Bryce calmly held up his watch. "Yeah, right where I thought it would be." He put it on. "Just checking to see if those red eyes would come back during the daytime."

"Well, I'm a little busy, so if you wouldn't mind . . ." He swept his arm toward the door.

We took the hint and hurried out.

CHAPTER 71

☺ *Bryce* ☺

"Mr. Rosel used that pulley to scare us away?" Ashley said as we headed back to the Konig estate.

"Maybe he does that to everybody. Or maybe it was someone else."

"But he was staying on the third floor. It had to be him."

"Unless there's someone else in the house," I said. "If he didn't want us there, why did he invite us?" I stomped the brake and the tires screeched.

"What?" Ashley said.

"I want to get a look at those stables. Maybe we'll see something."

When Ashley gets an idea, she expects everyone to follow like she's the Pied Piper. When I get an idea, I have to twist her arm and threaten to go alone, which I did. Finally she gave in.

We parked in a little turnaround, crossed the street, and crept into a small neighborhood of old houses. Soon we were in a wooded area behind The Broken Saber. Through the trees the house looked even more menacing.

The smell of the barn hit us. I've been to pig farms—those are the worst—but this was pretty bad. We slipped into the barn through a back door and tiptoed past the stalls. The three horses inside moved away as we passed. Their water troughs were empty, and there was no feed.

"Look at their hooves," Ashley said.

I squinted in the dim light. Their hooves had grown so much that they were turning up at the end.

Ashley found water and I found feed, and we stocked their troughs. Suddenly they weren't afraid. They ate and drank quickly, looking at us like they wanted to thank us. Ashley stroked their noses.

We found a spot where we could watch the house. Something was going on there, but what?

"Maybe Rosel isn't really dealing in books," I said. "Maybe he's hollowed them out and he's selling drugs or stolen gold or something."

Ashley looked at me like I had six heads and one of them was on fire. "If he's doing that, why would he invite us to his place?"

"Maybe he thought Mom was cute."

"So why would he scare the living peanuts out of us with those red eyes?"

"What are living peanuts?" I said.

She punched my arm. The waterfall chugged in the distance. A few cars passed, but mostly everything was peaceful.

"Where's the exterminator?" Ashley said.

I shook my head. "Must be late." I wondered if service people liked coming to The Broken Saber. Who would? "Ash, remember what Pastor Shepherd said about Jake getting back to his roots—the inspiration for his stories? Could Jake have gone to The Broken Saber—?"

She put a hand on my arm and pointed. Mr. Rosel and a woman came out the back door, moving quickly toward the barn. It looked like she was chewing him out. As they drew closer, she came clearly into view.

Caroline!

CHAPTER 72

❀ Ashley ❀

Bryce and I raced out the back and moved to the north side of the barn. With our backs to the old boards and peeling paint, we waited and listened.

"... told you not to get them involved," Caroline said. Her voice sure sounded different than the way she talked at the Konigs' place.

"I had to," Rosel said. "Don't you see? It's the final link to him. Now that it's gone—"

"But they'll call the police. And if they go to the book room ..."

"Nothing's going to happen. Those people were scared to death."

"Then why did the kids come back?"

"He left his watch, that's all. They're gone."

When they opened the door, Caroline wailed, "You told me you'd take care of the horses! Look at them!"

Bryce and I darted a good 50 yards into the woods and stopped in a pine grove.

"They were in on it together," Bryce said. "Caroline must have taken the disk from Mom's purse. I'll bet the disk and the manuscript are hidden in the book room."

"We're not going down there," I said. "We should just call the police. Besides, we don't know the combination."

"You said the first three numbers were 4-1-7. Jake's birthday is April 17. The last two numbers must be the year he was born."

"Nice. So Rosel, Caroline, and Pastor Shepherd are all in on this?"

"I don't know, but we have to get the manuscript and the disk back."

CHAPTER 73

⊘ *Bryce* ⊘

We ran for the road, then up the front steps of The Broken Saber. The door was locked.

"Come on," Ashley said, "let's call the police."

I turned. "Call them yourself," I said, knowing she didn't have a phone. "I'm going inside."

I stayed low and went around to the back door. I hurried up the steps and opened the creaky door. Ashley was right behind me, and we dashed inside.

We stayed on our hands and knees, looking out at the barn

through the screen, gasping, my heart beating like a toy drum. There was no movement out there.

We scuttled through the kitchen and into the sitting room. Finally we stood, and I raced Ashley down the stairs, two at a time. I punched the first four numbers on the keypad to the book room, but I messed up and it beeped at me.

"Make it good this time," Ashley said. "An alarm could go off."

I hit the Reset button and slowly punched the five numbers of Jake Konig's birth date. Bingo.

As soon as we were inside, I had to go to the bathroom. Bad. I closed my eyes and took a short breath.

Someone groaned. Or was it a door opening upstairs?

Ashley leaned closer. "I don't like this."

The voice again. It sounded a million miles away, echoing through the heating vent. "Ash," I whispered, "that's what I heard the other night. Someone calling for help."

CHAPTER 74

❀ Ashley ❀

I grabbed Bryce's cell phone and left to call the police, but I couldn't get a signal, even when I climbed the stairs. I said a bad word. It just slipped out. "Forgive me, Lord," I said, "and help me."

I tried the phone again with shaking hands. Then I heard voices from the kitchen. It was Caroline and Mr. Rosel.

I knew it. We should have left when we had the chance.

CHAPTER 75

◉ *Bryce* ◉

Jake's book covers scared me. One was a hand holding a huge knife dripping blood. Another showed the eyes and slithering tongue of a snake. Another had a ventriloquist's dummy terrorizing an audience.

I started pulling out books one by one, looking behind them and putting them back in. I started hopping around, trying to make the bathroom feeling go away.

Something banged and echoed through the walls, like in *The Count of Monte Cristo.* I moved to the back wall, shoved some books out of the way, and put my ear to the shelf. Something was moving inside—or was it underneath?

I dropped to the floor and put my ear to the soft dark green carpet. The tapping became clearer. Someone spoke, but the voice was muffled through the rug. On my hands and knees I carefully went over every inch, looking and feeling for anything strange. The edges were tacked down tight.

In the center of the room a small square table with a few books on top sat above an electrical plug in the floor. I slid the table to one side and knelt again. I found a seam in the carpet. The electrical box sat slightly above the floor line, so I grabbed it and pulled.

Nothing.

I noticed a sliding latch beside the electrical box. I slid it open and pulled up.

A section of the floor moved.

CHAPTER 76

❅ Ashley ❅

The only place I could hide was behind one of the huge chairs near the fireplace. If Mr. Rosel and Caroline went upstairs, they would have to pass me, and I was sunk. I heard them stop in the kitchen and pull chairs out from the table.

"Listen, this will soon be over," Mr. Rosel said. "Jake will make the changes, his body will be found, and then we'll discover his final manuscript."

"I don't see how you're going to pull it off."

"He's not well, Caroline. You heard the tapes. He's talking nonsense, searching for God, and all that. We're doing him a favor, salvaging his legacy. Who knows what would happen if he stayed on this course?"

Caroline sighed. "I keep thinking about his family. I wish you'd never gotten me into this in the first place."

Bryce's phone vibrated. If I hit the Answer button, it would beep, and I was afraid Rosel and Caroline would hear it.

"You know what kind of man he is," Mr. Rosel said. "His wife and son will be better off without him."

The chairs in the kitchen moved, and my heart fluttered. I flattened myself to the floor and could see Mr. Rosel's feet as he stood. "Help me tidy the rooms upstairs," he said.

CHAPTER 77

◑ *Bryce* ◑

When I lifted the electric box, a latch released and a two-foot-by-three-foot section of the floor came with it, leaving a rectangle big enough to crawl through. The floor section was heavy and seemed reinforced on the bottom. I set it aside and looked down the black hole. I imagined a million spiders smiling, rubbing their legs, and hoping I would join them.

"Anybody down there?" I said in a hoarse whisper. My voice echoed.

"Help!" a man said faintly. "Please help me!"

I slid back and let the light from the room hit the hole. The bottom of the shaft was only a few feet down. I put my feet over the edge, took a breath, and let myself down. I thought about pulling the floor section over the opening, but that would shut out all the light. No way was I going to do that.

When I reached the bottom I could almost stand up straight. A dim light shone ahead of me. I stayed crouched and moved toward the light, each step like walking a tightrope over Niagara Falls.

The tunnel was cool and damp and smelled musty. I wanted to feel the walls to guide me, but I was afraid of grabbing something alive.

"Please don't leave me," the man said. His cough sounded like a child's rattle.

"I'm coming," I whispered, trying to sound confident.

Something scurried in front of me, and I jumped back into a spiderweb. I flailed at my face, then brushed my shoulders and chest to make sure I didn't have any passengers.

The tunnel came to a T and I turned left. The ceiling pitched higher, and the ground angled down so I could finally stand. The farther I went, the more light I saw, and finally I was out of the tunnel and into a sparse room. A bare bulb hung from the ceiling over what looked like an old kitchen table. A cot sat in the corner not far from a tall, white bucket. (I didn't want to think about what the bucket was for, but I could smell it.) A man with a scraggly beard and wild hair sat at the table. His eyes grew wide and he tried to speak, but he only coughed.

One ankle was fitted with a chain hooked to the floor. It looked like he had just enough chain to get to the cot, the table, or the bucket. On the table lay a pile of papers.

"Jake?" I said.

He stared. "I don't know who you are, kid, but you have to get me out of here."

CHAPTER 78

✖ Ashley ✖

The footsteps came close, right to the chair, and I hunkered down. The phone rang in the kitchen. Mr. Rosel stopped inches from me and turned back. Caroline sighed and sat heavily in the chair.

"Who is it?" Caroline called out as the phone rang again.

"It's coming from the Konig estate."

The phone rang and rang. I wanted to scream "Pick it up!"

Finally Rosel did. "Yes, ma'am, they were here for your son's watch and went on their way. . . ."

He hung up and came back to the living room.

"Something happen with those twins?" Caroline said.

She said "those twins" like we were dead skunks.

"Mommy is worried. I predict all three of them will be gone by this afternoon. I accomplished that last night."

"How did you keep him quiet while they were here?"

"Gave him a shot before they arrived, then another after midnight. They heard him, but I convinced them it was my television."

"What if they don't leave?"

Mr. Rosel laughed, and it gave me chills. "Let's get those rooms ready in case the authorities show up," he said.

The chair moved.

I had to do something or they would see me.

CHAPTER 79

◎ *Bryce* ◎

Jake Konig didn't look like the scary author I'd seen on television. He looked sick—like a man on a deserted island. Only this island was underground and about 20 degrees cooler than above ground. To be honest, he looked afraid.

He started with questions. "Who are you? How'd you get down here? How'd you find me? Does anybody else know you're here?"

"My sister is calling my mom right now." Just talking with him made the bathroom feeling go away.

"She ought to call the police. Do you have a cell phone?"

"My sister has it. We couldn't get a signal down here anyway."

"Of course we couldn't, not down . . . sister . . ." He stared at me like something had suddenly clicked. "You're Kathryn's boy, aren't you?"

I nodded and stuck out my hand. "I'm Bryce."

He didn't reach for my hand. "I wouldn't touch me if I were you, but it's good to see you. So Kathryn *is* working on my book."

I knelt to inspect the chain. "Was, until it was stolen. Like everybody else, Ashley and I have been trying to figure out where you went."

The chain was hooked to a thick metal sleeve that fit over Mr. Konig's ankle. It would have taken me a year to hacksaw through the chain—if I had a hacksaw—and the sleeve wasn't coming off without a key. Mr. Konig's leg was bloody under his pant leg.

"The only way I can get out is if you get the cops here," he said. "And if Rosel finds you, we're both dead."

CHAPTER 80

✖ Ashley ✖

I closed my eyes and held my breath as Mr. Rosel and Caroline passed. When the stairs creaked, I peeked. They were heading up to the rooms.

I stayed still, not moving a molecule.

Suddenly Mr. Rosel looked down, directly at me, and his face twisted like some Jake Konig character.

I waved. "Hi there."

He shot past Caroline and barreled down the stairs.

I had two options. Run and scream my head off or stand my ground. I pulled out Bryce's cell phone. "What's she doing here?" I said, pointing to Caroline. Mr. Rosel stopped at the bottom of the stairs. "You and Caroline have done something with Mr. Konig, haven't you? One phone call will bring the police."

"Earl, where's the boy?" Caroline said.

When I glanced up at her Mr. Rosel lunged for me and knocked the phone to the floor. He scrambled after it, and I headed for the kitchen. When I reached the phone, I heard someone behind me, whirled, and saw Caroline.

I dodged her, and she slid on the slick floor into the counter. I had to get to a phone, but I also had to keep them away from Bryce. I hurried back to where Mr. Rosel stood with the cell phone, looking at the display—it must have been vibrating. I ran straight for him, then veered around the chair and raced up the stairs. "Bryce, I'm coming!"

Caroline and Mr. Rosel followed, but I ducked into the Jake Konig room, slammed the door, and locked it.

"Where's the key?" Caroline said.

"Downstairs. I'll get it."

There was no phone in the room. I was trapped, but I still had to keep them from finding Bryce.

"They're behind me, Bryce," I said. "Can we get out the window?"

"Shh," I said, hoping they'd think that was Bryce.

CHAPTER 81

◎ *Bryce* ◎

It was as if Jake Konig and I were in a soundproof chamber.
The walls were dirt and tree roots stuck through, but the place
seemed surprisingly clean. I wondered how Mr. Rosel had gotten
electricity down here.

I told Jake what had been happening and said, "Why did Mr. Rosel
do this?"

"He's crazy. He'd read all my books, asked me to sign a bunch of
them, but I said no." He coughed. "I only sign for bookstores or private collectors, not for individuals trying to make money off me. I
should have known something was up when I heard he was selling

autographed copies. He even wanted me to read his writing, but I don't have time to start doing that for everybody. Then I was coming back from the diner after a meeting—"

"With Pastor Shepherd?"

"Yeah. And things started getting fuzzy. I pulled to the side of the road. I got off my cycle and collapsed. When I woke up, I was here. Rosel must have been in the diner, put something in my food or coffee."

Rosel must have been the one who called the pastor's beeper too.

"What have you been doing here all this time?" I said.

"He has me reworking my new book. I keep a copy with me, and at first he let me use a computer. He was stupid enough to let me use one with a built-in wireless connection. I accessed my computer at home, but he was monitoring me. As soon as I sent a message asking for help, he yanked the computer and made me work with a pen."

"So he was the one who sent us the warnings."

"Did he?"

I nodded. "Why didn't he like your story?"

"He said it was too religious. Said he wasn't going to let me switch sides, whatever that means."

"Maybe he thought you were going to become a Christian. But how would he know anything about that?"

"He told me he planted a microphone in the booth at the diner."

So that was how he knew about Mom's disk and the manuscript. He'd heard us with Pastor Shepherd.

CHAPTER 82

❀ Ashley ❀

"Ashley and Bryce, come out here," Caroline said. "This is not what you think."

I heard tires on gravel and moved to the back window as Caroline kept urging us to come out. Clancy had pulled into the driveway on the golf cart. I threw open the window and put a finger to my lips. "Caroline and Rosel have done something with your dad!" I whispered.

"I'll get the police."

"No time! Help us get out of here."

Clancy looked toward the house, then backed away from the golf cart. Rosel was approaching him.

"The barn!" I yelled. "Head for the barn!"

Clancy took off, and there was no way Rosel could catch him. This was my chance to help Bryce.

CHAPTER 83

◑ *Bryce* ◑

I had dreamed of meeting Jake Konig, but never this way.
Not in a dungeon. This was not cool. I looked around the room for
any way out, but the only way out seemed to be back through the
darkness.

I heard someone in the book room. It had to be Ashley. Or maybe
she'd called the police.

"Hey!" I yelled. "We're down here!" I ran through the tunnel,
bent over into the darkness. Jake's chain clanked and he yelped.

I headed for the opening. "Ashley?"

Caroline's face appeared and I stopped. She shook her head. "You don't know what you've done." She covered the opening and the latch clicked.

I beat on the bottom, but when I heard the book-room door close, I went back to Jake.

"Kathryn will find you," he said. "You know, we met back in Chicago when we were young. I—"

"I'd love to hear this sometime, but I have to get out of here."

He pointed to a corner. "Look behind those boards. It must lead somewhere because I feel air coming through there sometimes."

The boards were weathered like they'd been there since the gold rush. I knocked on them, and the sound was hollow. I pulled at one and it cracked.

"There you go," Jake said. "Yank it out of there."

It took a few minutes, but when I finally removed the boards I couldn't see into the inky blackness.

I stood on the table and unhooked the lightbulb cord from a bent nail in the support beam. The cord reached the corner, and I pointed the light into the darkness. "The shaft continues," I said. "I have to try it."

"It's risky, kid. What if there's a drop-off or you get caught?" He looked at the floor.

"I have to try. How else are you going to—?"

"I'd never forgive myself if—I mean, I've already screwed up my own son."

"Clancy. Watched a movie with him the other night. He's nice."

"He's doing all right? And my wife?"

"They're just worried sick about you. Look, this might be our only chance."

"I don't like it," Konig said. "You should—"

"No," I said. "Remember in *Chasing the Dead* where you had

the parents always telling their son he couldn't do stuff, couldn't make a difference, couldn't accomplish anything? The kid fought the monster and saved the town."

Konig sat there nodding, seeming to look at me with new eyes. "Then go get the monster, Bryce. And don't forget me."

CHAPTER 84

❁ Ashley ❁

I listened at the door but couldn't hear Caroline. I took a chance and unlocked it, eased the door open, and stepped into the hall, quietly shutting the door. I scanned the sitting room and watched the kitchen as I moved toward the stairs.

Footsteps.

Caroline appeared in the kitchen and paused. "Earl?" When he didn't answer, she headed upstairs. I eased around a corner and held my breath. When she reached the top, she turned toward the Jake Konig room, knocked, called my name, then tried the knob.

The door swung open. "Ashley? Bryce?" When she stepped inside,

I hurried down the stairs as quietly as I could, but I knew she could hear me. She yelled, but I kept going. Through the kitchen door I saw Mr. Rosel running for the house. Clancy was nowhere in sight.

I hit the door to the basement and bounded down the stairs. I punched the combination, flew into the book room, and turned on the lights. "Bryce?"

He wasn't there.

CHAPTER 85

☻ *Bryce* ☻

I couldn't see a thing and took each step like I was testing for land mines.

Where was Ashley? Mom? Would Dylan and Sam and Leigh ever know what became of us?

Something crackled, and bits of dirt and rock showered me. I thought the tunnel roof was coming down. The shaft took a sharp turn, and I could feel that I had come to a fork.

I was going to have to make a choice. Right or left?

CHAPTER 86

✖ Ashley ✖

I loved seeing Mr. Rosel's eyes when he saw I was in the book room. He punched the code and threw open the door, but he and Caroline stopped. His eyes grew wide, and he held out both hands. "Now, young lady, put that down. Th-this is a big misunderstanding. There's no reason to—"

"Stop," I said, holding the pages from the velvet-lined box. "One more step and I tear these to pieces."

"Those are priceless. . . ."

"Then stay where you are."

"Ashley," Caroline said, "don't do anything rash."

"Put the cell phone on the floor and go upstairs," I said.

Rosel hesitated.

I shifted the pages, ready to tear them.

"No!" Mr. Rosel said. He threw the phone to the floor. "We'll go."

They retreated out the door and up the steps. I picked up the phone and followed, still holding the pages. Mr. Rosel kept looking over his shoulder to make sure I wasn't tearing his precious pages.

"Sit," I said when we got to the kitchen, and they sat. I called Mom and told her to bring the police.

CHAPTER 87

⊙ *Bryce* ⊙

The left fork was a dead end—just a big, earthen wall. I worked my way back to the fork and took the other path. I was going faster now, not as careful as when I started.

I heard something behind me and stopped. I turned back and walked a few yards, feeling another tunnel. A gust of wind whipped my face. That had to be the way out. I plunged blindly into the dark. I spotted a tree root dangling and ducked. *Hey, I can see!*

Please, God, I prayed, *help me get out of here.*

Ahead was what looked like a nest, lots of leaves and branches mashed together. Two eyes stared at me, not like the red ones from the night before. These were cute and cuddly, with pointed ears on each side. Whatever it was jumped and scampered away—and then another and another.

Foxes! God sent foxes to lead me out!

I followed them, and sure enough I spied a small hole ahead with light peeking through. The foxes darted out and disappeared. Now if I could just make the hole big enough to squeeze through.

CHAPTER 88

❈ Ashley ❈

Mr. Rosel and Caroline sat there with smug looks, as if they knew they could explain everything to the authorities. I rummaged in the cupboards and found matches and a candle. I lit it and held the pages close.

"Where's Bryce?" I said.

"I haven't seen him," Mr. Rosel said.

I held the pages closer to the flame, and he sat forward. "Honestly, I don't know where he is."

"He went to the book room," I said.

Mr. Rosel glanced at Caroline, then looked at the floor.

"What about Clancy?" I said.

"I couldn't catch him. Please give me the pages and we'll work this out."

"Stay where you are or you'll be scraping ashes off the floor."

A police car pulled into the driveway with its lights flashing. Mom was next, driven by Gerald.

I ran outside, knowing I was safe but worried sick over Bryce.

"Officer, she was trying to steal my valuable papers," Mr. Rosel said from behind me, snatching the pages from my hand.

"That's a lie!" I yelled, turning to Mom. "Bryce is still in there somewhere."

"Where's my son?" Mom said.

"I saw him running that way." Mr. Rosel pointed toward town. "He was trying to steal—"

The officer put up a hand. "Let's step inside and sort this out."

Mr. Rosel got mushy as we walked up the steps. "This was just a misunderstanding. I'm willing to forgive and forget without pressing charges."

"I want my son," Mom said.

"I told you, I saw him running—"

Clancy came in the kitchen door. "My dad has to be here somewhere. I found his motorcycle under a tarp in the barn. It's been stripped, but I'd recognize it anywhere."

Mr. Rosel shook his head. "That's not your father's. I can assure you, it's mine."

"Then why are you hiding it?" Clancy said.

"It was supposed to be a surprise. Caroline and I have been seeing each other. She mentioned how much she liked your father's bike, so I bought one just like it for her birthday."

"Don't listen to him, Clancy," I said, noticing that Caroline had disappeared. "They've done something with your dad. I heard them talking about him. Maybe Bryce found him. Come on."

I raced to the third floor. Mr. Rosel's room was furnished simply with an antique dresser and bed. In the corner, next to the window, stood a tall closetlike cabinet. I slid open a drawer.

Red eyes stared back at me.

I jumped back.

Clancy held up the rubber eyes that looked human. They were connected to a thin wire that coiled around a spindle.

"So you've discovered my secret," Mr. Rosel said.

I whipped around, holding the eyes. "You thought you could scare us away with these?"

"Not scare you away," he said, smiling. "Just raise your blood pressure with those and the sounds I played through the hidden speakers throughout the house. Most guests love how it gets their imaginations going."

Clancy said, "Where's my dad?"

"I have no idea what you're talking about, young man. And I don't like the accusation."

Clancy pushed past him, and I followed Clancy down the stairs. The police officer stood near the kitchen, talking on his radio.

Mom was next to him. "Get off there and help me find my son."

"You're sure the last you saw of the boy he was heading toward town, Mr. Rosel?" the officer said. "Nobody's seen him."

Rosel shrugged. "I'm sorry I didn't get his flight plan. He *was* trying to steal from me. Perhaps he's hiding somewhere, ashamed."

The officer said, "It seems we have a lot more questions than answers." He turned to Mom. "Let's head to the Konig estate and see if your son turns up."

"No!" I said. "Bryce is still here!"

Mom pulled me toward the door. "Let's get Gerald and see if we can find him."

"Wait!" We turned to see someone in the living room, mud-streaked and looking a little like Bigfoot. But it wasn't.

It was Bryce.

CHAPTER 89

☺ *Bryce* ☺

Mom and Ashley ran to me, and the police officer stared. "Where've you been, son?" he said.

"I'll show you," I said. I turned to Mr. Rosel. "Where's the key to Jake's chain?"

He smirked. "I don't know what you're talking about."

I tromped mud through the sitting room and down the stairs as the officer kept a grip on Rosel's arm. Ashley punched the combination to the book room.

I moved the table and pulled up the opening. "He's down here. Chained by the ankle. Where's the key?"

Mr. Rosel rolled his eyes.

The police officer searched the man's pockets and found keys. "I don't want to leave the suspect up here," the cop said.

"Then give me the keys," I said. "Mr. Konig is sick and shouldn't be left there another minute."

Jake began yelling as soon as he heard me, and he looked at me like I was his long-lost best friend. When I unlocked the cuff, Jake sprinted for the opening, staggering and falling.

I grabbed the manuscript from the table and followed. "Help him up!" I called from behind.

Mom reached for him and I pushed, and as soon as Jake got through the hole in the floor, he tried to attack Rosel. The man whimpered and hid behind the officer like a terrified kitten.

"We'll take care of him, sir," the cop said. "You'd better sit down."

Two more officers arrived. One took Rosel away, and the other went looking for Caroline.

"I can't thank your son and daughter enough, Kathryn," Jake said. "I don't think I would have lasted much longer. Now I just want to see my family."

CHAPTER 90

❀ Ashley ❀

It doesn't take much to make me cry. A sappy movie. "The Star-Spangled Banner" or "God Bless America." Puppies being rescued.

When Clancy walked in and saw his father, all it took was one word: *Dad.* I lost it.

Jake Konig melted in that room, surrounded by his life's work—scary books that had led him into a prison—and his son. I could tell by the way they hugged that things were going to work out, and I hoped the same would be true for Jake and his wife. When we finally got back to his estate, Lorie Konig actually cried.

At dinner that night Jake had shaved and changed into clean clothes, but he sure looked exhausted. His doctor had given him some medicine for his cough but said he would be okay. Camera crews camped at the end of the driveway, and Gerald held them at bay.

After dinner, Gerald called to say he had let one car through.

A few minutes later Pastor Shepherd rushed in and hugged Jake. "I've been praying for you."

"That means a lot," Jake said.

"I thought Hank Clashman had stolen the manuscript. That's why I asked you to hold off on calling the police. I wish I could say Hank's a changed man." He looked at Mom. "You might want to prepare for his protesting your books too."

"I can handle it," she said.

"The police found your disk and the manuscript stolen from my office. Earl Rosel is in deep trouble."

CHAPTER 91

☺ *Bryce* ☺

Dylan looked like he had grown two inches, and Leigh looked like she had spent a year at hard labor camp. Her face lit up when Mom calculated all the hours and wrote her a check. "This should help you get a car."

I found out that the mine shaft I'd been in goes for miles. I might never have found my way out if I hadn't had help from those heavenly foxes.

Two days later Gerald showed up at our front door, smiling. He said the Konigs had gone on a vacation together to some deserted island. Caroline had been caught and confessed to her part in Rosel's scheme.

Gerald handed Mom an envelope and said it was a token of thanks from Jake for her work on his book, with a little added for Ashley and me for saving his life.

Earl Rosel went to jail for a bunch of years, conspiracy to commit a felony and unlawful imprisonment being the major charges. Caroline got less time because she cooperated.

A farmer took the neglected horses from The Broken Saber and soon had them doing fine. Hank Clashman left the church and moved away, probably somewhere where he found something else to protest.

Jake's new book came out six months later. It had his usual rough language in it, but the critics said it was his best and called it "redemptive," "compelling," and "riveting." Mom talked with Jake a lot and also kept in touch with Pastor Shepherd. The pastor said he and Jake were still meeting regularly and that Jake was working on mending his family. As for his relationship with God, Pastor Shepherd said, "Jake's not there yet, but he's on the journey."

Clancy e-mails Ashley every now and then. Turned out his dad didn't want him to go back to Wildmore anyway. Clancy's going to one of the local schools in Shadow Falls and says he likes taking a creative-writing class. His dad teaches a seminar there once a month. Clancy isn't a Christian yet either, but Ashley and I are both praying for him.

I'm still a Jake Konig fan, but I've stopped reading the Dead End series. I figure life isn't really a dead end if you hang in there and work at it.

Mom showed me the first page of Jake's new adult book. It reads: *To Bryce and Ashley. Lifesavers.*

About the Authors

Jerry B. Jenkins (jerryjenkins.com) is the writer of the Left Behind series. He owns the Jerry B. Jenkins Christian Writers Guild, an organization dedicated to mentoring aspiring authors. Former vice president for publishing for the Moody Bible Institute of Chicago, he also served many years as editor of *Moody* magazine and is now Moody's writer-at-large.

His writing has appeared in publications as varied as *Reader's Digest, Parade, Guideposts,* in-flight magazines, and dozens of other periodicals. Jenkins's biographies include books with Billy Graham, Hank Aaron, Bill Gaither, Luis Palau, Walter Payton, Orel Hershiser, and Nolan Ryan, among many others. His books appear regularly on the *New York Times, USA Today, Wall Street Journal,* and *Publishers Weekly* best-seller lists.

Jerry is also the writer of the nationally syndicated sports story comic strip *Gil Thorp,* distributed to newspapers across the United States by Tribune Media Services.

Jerry and his wife, Dianna, live in Colorado and have three grown sons and three grandchildren.

Chris Fabry is a writer and broadcaster who lives in Colorado. He has written more than 40 books, including collaboration on the Left Behind: The Kids series.

You may have heard his voice on Focus on the Family, Moody Broadcasting, or Love Worth Finding. He has also written for Adventures in Odyssey and Radio Theatre.

Chris is a graduate of the W. Page Pitt School of Journalism at Marshall University in Huntington, West Virginia. He and his wife, Andrea, have been married 22 years and have nine children, two birds, two dogs, and one cat.